Snow Blood

Season 1: Episodes 1 - 6

By

Carol McKibben

www.trollriverpub.com
Snow Blood
Season 1: Episodes 1 - 6
Copyright © 2014 Carol McKibben
ISBN: 978-1-939564-36-8

Dear Reader,

Carol has worked very hard on this particular piece of entertainment. This book was brought to you by hard labor and love. Please respect an artist's work for the enrichment we try to bring you. I humbly ask that you don't outright steal this child born on paper and brought to you by love. If you come by this book by nefarious means, and you are simply unable to give the change in your pocket for the purchase price, then take it with my blessing. But if you can purchase it and would like Carol to continue to bring you great books, please purchase a copy to support her.

Thank you,

Troll River Publications

EPISODE ONE
Transformation

The pain sliced into my ribs like steel on bone. Then, nothingness.

Searing pain, and the sight of two snarling, rabid beasts locked in battle, interrupted the safety of my void. The scent of their blood-filled rage made my nose twitch. My brain screamed "move" but my legs disobeyed. Paralyzed on the ground, I watched as two giant beasts circled each other, lumbering dangerously close. One, an unknown, unnatural brother who could stand on hind legs. The other ... a demon, perhaps? That was the best way I could describe this otherworldly creature.

My eyes began to focus. I could see blood-covered fangs and claws, a demon strangely glowing in the lunar light. It looked "moon-kissed". Light from the night-time sun caressed this deformed creature. Perhaps I'm imagining this? Maybe it's my love of the moon. I've always felt its protection at night on my forays into the woods near my home.

Jaws snapping. The upright wolf-being lunged. The demon creature moved faster, almost a blur. It hastily side-stepped the wolf's bite as easily as a mongoose avoids a cobra. The wolf snarled its frustration. It circled the moon-kissed demon that appeared to be taunting its opponent. I tried to move to observe better, but pain savagely raked through me. A dark circle of wetness surrounded me. The air reeked with the smell of ... blood. My blood.

Why had I recklessly left the comfort of my home? The fireplace in the den warmed us against the outside of fall's cold weather. Perhaps I needed adventure. Prey lurked in the outside darkness, and instinctively, I had wanted to give chase. My little human tried to tackle me just as I dashed to the kitchen and nosed aside the flap from the back door to the freedom of the night that beckoned me.

"Snow! Don't go out there. It's dark!" He squirmed, trying to hold me. He weighed less than any little subaltern laying his body across my shaggy mass. Embarrassing, I thought, since I outranked him in the pack. But, I never snapped at him. My little human needed my protection.

"Let him go, Tommy. He's just doing his job; keeping the coyotes away." Tommy's father, our Alpha, had spoken, and we must all obey.

The little human stood upright and slowly released his grip on my back. Moments later, I was chasing coyotes across the front lawn and out into the street, doing what I did best – protecting my pack. Now, as the sound of gnashing teeth brought me back into the present, I wished for the chance to better safeguard them. Who would warn my humans of this danger if I didn't make it home?

The two creatures battled on. The wolf leaped over its combatant's head, narrowly avoiding a crushing blow to its leg. The glowing demon blurred, quickly avoiding an attack from the rear. It spun just in time to avoid its throat from being taken. Suddenly, fall leaves were flying into the air. They hit the grass under the trees that lined the abandoned road and tumbled, arms and heads over legs.

My paws quivered as the fight drew closer to me. Inexplicitly, I remained unable to move from where I had landed after the pain hit me. My energy had already seeped from my body. Running away appeared no longer an option.

I watched as the fierce beasts arose quickly from their tumble. The wolf gained an advantage, lunging forward and extending its claws as the demon stumbled over a broken tree trunk. Its opportune fall to the ground enabled the demon to duck the razor-sharp claws. Just missing the demon, the wolf landed and rolled behind its enemy. Quickly, it spun up to go after its prey now sprawled out on the grass.

Just as the wolf leaped, BOOM. A loud explosion ... and then the wolf crumpled to the ground with a pained yelp and a heavy thud. His lifeless body sprawled awkwardly on the dirt.

A strange voice pierced through my head. "Silver bullets work well on panweres, too." A malicious chuckle followed.

Was that the demon's voice? I wondered. Surely I did not see his lips moving.

The demon creature knelt over its victim and poked the wolf's body. No sign of life. Triumphantly, it threw back its head and let out a victory scream that made the hairs on my neck bristle. It then rose to cast its appraising gaze in my direction. I struggled to get my feet under me, fearing that if I didn't, the demon would kill me on this spot, just as he had taken the life of the wolf. As it approached me, I felt my life slowly drain away; the darkness enveloped me again. The sadness of never seeing my family again lingered ...

Darkness closed over me ... drifting into ... an overwhelming itchy sensation? My nerve endings were on fire, consuming me with a new-found rush. The thin line of life spread throughout me. Every fiber of my body stood on end as the blood-filled eyes of the demon pierced mine. A thin drop of blood clung to one of its fangs before descending onto my face in slow motion. I tried to move but the creature held me in place with one giant claw-covered hand. Other than the weight of its massive body, I felt no trace of the initial pain that had sent me into darkness.

I watched transfixed as the creature transformed into a human. First claws became large hands. It shrunk only slightly. Its deformed body took the shape of a strong, muscular athlete. Its distorted visage faded into a handsome face with a strong nose, cheek bones, and jaw. It was only seconds until it became a naked man. It spoke. "Hold still, dog. Let your body absorb my venom and heal."

Venom? Heal me? Fire streaked through my veins, forcing every part of me to come alive. An unfamiliar strength enveloped me. I had been crippled only moments ago. Now, every part of me sprang to life. My eyes never left the demon/man.

Blond and fair, a pale face framed large violet-colored eyes that transitioned back to red and again to violet. He towered over me; his long, muscular frame stretched over what must have been almost a half-head taller than James, my master. I once heard my master brag, "I'm six-foot-one in my stocking feet." I guess that was his way of stating how tall he is.

The demon/man wiped the blood from his face onto his hand. My blood, or his? I wasn't sure.

"All right," he commanded, "try to get up now."

I sprang to all fours, shook my heavy white coat and sat back on my haunches. How did I get on this deserted road in the middle of the woods? Prey. That's it. Chasing prey. The large black car with Oregon plates sitting sideways in the road next to us, lights on, motor running, looked as though it had swerved to avoid something. Had it collided with me?

The man knelt down and patted my head. "Confused are you? That's right, I hit you."

I cocked my head at him, feeling better than before. How could he have hit me? I got a whiff of his odor. A layer of perfume concealed the smell of death and something rotten that had emanated from the demon during its battle with the wolf. I stood and shook my whole body again, as if to expel the experience and the smell. Then I turned away to go back home.

"Wait!" He placed a firm grip on my back with his strong, human hands.

I whipped my head around, baring teeth in warning. Let me go! I had to go home to my loving family and the warm fire that awaited me.

He stared at me. "No, that's an insane thought."

Was he speaking to me? Was he reading my mind?

He paused for a long moment, staring at me as if he could see through me. I shivered from the menacing touch of his hand on my back.

He released his grip. His shoulders slumped, and he ran a bloody hand through his blond hair. He took a long, deep breath, then shook his head. "Come with me."

I watched him move toward the car. I had to go home. My people must be worried.

He turned to me, and I felt drawn to him. No, I must go home.

"There is no choice, dog. Come with me."

No! The hackles on my back stood on end in warning. I will go home! I backed away, growling in defiance. I turned to run, but he blocked my path to freedom and caught me in a heartbeat.

He stopped me in my tracks. How could this human outrun me?

He grabbed my head with his bloody hands and twisted my face to meet his blood-red eyes. "You will come with me now! It is for your survival and that of your people." He let go and stood tall again. He took two long strides to the car. Over his shoulder he commanded, "Come!"

I resisted with everything that I had.

He opened a door to the large sedan and motioned for me to take the passenger seat. I tried to resist again but my legs disobeyed me, and I covered the short space and jumped in. He slammed the door behind me.

I growled as I watched him cross in front of the car and open the driver's door. A black turtleneck sweater and black pants hung on the back of the driver's seat. Black loafers and socks sat on the floor in front of the seat. He reached inside for them and hurriedly put them on, never taking his eyes from me. His gaze was creeping me out. Intense.

Sliding behind the wheel, he looked at me for a long minute. "You're my responsibility now. Let's go find you something to eat. You will need your strength."

I didn't like his toothy grin. What wasn't he telling me?

I found it odd that my ravenous cravings for something ... something very bloody outweighed all other reason.

*****

I spat out the bitter meat after sucking every drop of blood from it. What is wrong with me? I had always

7

devoured a good piece of meat with joy. This brought none, just a bitterness that only the blood from it could mask. The smell repulsed me. Nauseated, I nudged it away.

I looked around me, trying not to think of my pack, or my growing hunger. The surroundings were elegant. Where are we?

"At my wine estate in Chehalem Valley, not far from Newburg." He sat, his legs crossed, in a large, overstuffed mahogany chair covered in maroon velvet pulled near a giant fireplace.

My pack lives in Newburg, Oregon. I crept closer to the fire, but it gave me no warmth. I felt neither warmth nor cold, just hunger. He stared at me with those large eyes that seemed to shift from purple to red, and then back to purple. He appeared deep in thought. His raspy voice surprised me.

"Meat will no longer work for you, dog. You need blood, and soon, to complete your transformation." He sipped from a large glass, savoring the red liquid on his tongue after he spoke.

Transformation? The word made me shiver.

"But, before I take you hunting, what shall I call you?"

I remained silent.

"Come here." The man's eyes bore into me.

My resolve to disobey dissolved.

I walked to him.

He bent down and looked deeply into my eyes. "What is your name?"

My thoughts betrayed me as my legs had earlier. I felt compelled to answer. *My name is Snow.*

"Ah, yes. Snow. I shall call you Snow ... Blood. You can call me Brogio."

I heard the words, but his mouth didn't move.

He took another sip from his glass and smiled. "That's right; you're hearing my thoughts. Spoken words will not be needed between us now." He held up his glass.

I wondered what was in the glass.

"This is wine from my winery. Vintage 1985."

I was relieved that he wasn't drinking a glass of blood in front of me. *So tell me, Brogio, why do we not need words?*

Again, the smile. The eyes turned deep red for a fraction of a second. A cold chill coursed through me, and I shivered. I wanted to run, but where? This Brogio could outrun me. And he could read my mind too! Anger rose up, and I let out a reflexive growl.

"I am an Artemis. Animals understand and obey me. It is the way. And now, I am your sire."

If you control animals, why did the strange wolf attack you?

"I have no control over panweres."

Panweres? Never heard of them. What ...

"A shape shifter. A creature that can shift into many different kinds of animals." He stood straight up. "Come, you must feed. We can talk more later."

I want to go home.

"No, you can't. It would be dangerous." He kneeled down next to me. "Snow Blood, you would end up killing those you love until I can teach you to control your urges."

I shook my head from side to side. *I don't understand.*

He sighed and return to the oversized chair, taking a long drink of the remaining wine.

I sat firmly in place. I refused to go anywhere until I understood what he meant.

"Snow." He sat back in the chair as if ready to tell me a story, "You are becoming a vampire. And, only a vampire can make another." He stared at me to let the words sink in. "You died on the road, and I turned you to bring you back."

I died? I am dead? I didn't remember any of it. The shock of his words shook me to my core. *How can that be? I am fine!*

"Only because I healed you and brought you back." His gaze met mine, and I knew it was true. The darkness, the blood, my paralysis, the feeling of being revitalized. My coat still carried traces of dried blood. "The only way to save you was to make you a vampire."

What is a vampire?

"You are of the Kindred, the undead, and somewhat immortal. We don't appear to age. Many of us survive for centuries." He leaned forward. "Dog, I warn you. Vampirism is a curse; not a blessing.

Then why did you not let me die?

"Selfish reasons, I suppose."

What reasons?

Brogio ignored me. "Understand, it carries great power but has many detriments. Not the least of which is the rage of the beast. Oh, and feeding on human blood."

I sat stunned and motionless. I didn't know what detriments were, but the rest ... it sounded absolutely awful. Terrifying. I longed to go home and hear the voices of the ones I loved, James and Tommy and our female Alpha, Jeanne. I closed my eyes and imagined the kind stroke of their hands on my back. I loved my humans. They were my pack. I could never hurt them.

"Yes, you will hurt them," Brogio uttered, having read my thoughts. "For us, the act of feeding is euphoric. The human actually feels ecstatic when it happens, and you will undergo a rush." He stood up and began to pace. "I have struggled with this, and it pains me. Some vampires have sustained their undeath by drinking the blood of animals. They rarely do so for very long. The needs of their cursed bodies force them to seek human blood."

What then, if I bite my humans? Will they become vampires? I struggled with the knowledge that I could hurt them in any way. I had been with them since I left my litter.

11

Tommy, my constant companion, had become my best friend. James and Jeanne had spoiled me from the moment we met. They treated me as more family member than pet. I visualized them out in the woods calling my name, frantic that something had happened to me.

"A person doesn't become a vampire if he, or she, is bitten, or killed by us. It takes a conscious act of will. I call it the Embrace ... to create a new vampire." He stopped his pacing and looked at me for long seconds. He appeared to be in deep deliberation. Finally, he continued. "We can leave little to mark our passing if we are careful. All I have to do to hide the wound left by my feeding is to lick it when I'm done."

From his description, it sounded as if these vampires had great power, but also many unpleasant parts to their existence. I did not want to be one. It appeared I had little choice. Looking for something positive, I latched on to a question.

He answered before I could form further thoughts.

"Yes, I have many disciplines. I can turn into any form of animal. Sometimes I can fly. And I have the strength of a hundred men. Just a few of my ... attributes."

Will I be able to fly?

He laughed, and I cocked my head at him.

It's a serious question!

"I suppose we will discover that together. I have never sired a dog in all my time." He poured himself another glass of wine and returned to his large chair near the fire.

How long have you been training people to become vampires?

Brogio's glass paused mid-way to his lips, and he rolled his eyes and smirked at me.

Then, what are detriments?

"The bad side. In my case, I can't go out in the sun again. This will probably be the same for you. You'll evaporate if you do.

Then what do you do during the day?

"Sleep. Only the most resolute can shake it off. It's forced." He sighed, growing weary of my questions.

I can't sleep all day!

"Yes, you will. And don't get a stake run through your heart. It will put you down until it's removed."

Don't get meat put through my heart? How does that happen?

Again, he laughed. "No. Not a steak. A wooden stake. He pointed to a sharp object hanging on the wall. "Like that one over there."

Wow. That looks pretty scary. I wouldn't want to get stabbed with that. I was panting heavily, staring up at the sharp object. I wondered if there were any other vampire rules that I should know about. *Are there others?*

13

"You now know the important ones." He stood up impatiently.

"We must complete your transformation. You need blood, even if it is only the blood of an animal tonight."

I shuddered at the thought. Animals were for chasing, not blood. *What ...*

"Come, now! You will understand later."

*****

I resisted following him. I licked away the thick saliva pooling on my tongue and dripping from my mouth. My stomach knotted with hunger. I could think of nothing else.

Brogio threw his clothes and shoes onto his large chair by the fireplace, then morphed into a demon, eyes ablaze, fangs snarling, claws slashing. He growled and sprinted through the front door after yanking it almost off its hinges. I hesitated, but the hunger in every fiber of my being pushed me to follow.

I tried to catch him as he sprinted through the fields and into the trees. I had never seen another creature move that fast. When I caught up to him, he had snared a large rabbit and ripped its throat open. He sunk his fangs into the gaping hole, then offered it to me.

Frightened by my desire, I backed away. I fought the blood lust that consumed me until I could fight no longer. Letting go, I ripped the creature to shreds, sucking every drop of blood from its torn body. A momentary sense of euphoria spread through me ... but it passed quickly.

Brogio, the demon, snarled and willed me to follow along behind him deeper into the trees. Stopping abruptly, he froze as I pulled up short so as not to hit him. We waited silently and were rewarded as a large deer sprinted in front of us. The demon creature blurred before my eyes ... twenty times faster than my human master. Much faster than a speedy deer. It was a sight to behold.

Brogio hit the deer with such force that it was crushed to the ground before it could escape. The demon Brogio lay across the dazed deer, almost covering its struggling body. He stared into the animal's eyes until it stopped moving.

My thirst for blood grew even stronger. I crashed into the deer's neck, trying to push the demon out of the way with my front paws. But he easily overpowered me and grabbed me by my scruff. "Wait!"

I backed away and watched as he punctured the submissive animal's throat with a fang, then he stepped back and motioned for me to feed. His words filled my mind. "No need to mutilate it; use your fangs to suck the blood from the artery in its throat."

I approached, and a surge of energy charged through me. I bit into the deer's neck and drained its body. It consumed me with an ecstasy I had never known, even better than coupling with the stray bitches that had gotten loose in my neighborhood. I rolled over on my back and surrendered to the orgasmic waves rolling through me.

The demon's rough voice in my head praised me. "Good! That will help until we feast on humans!"

Humans? We were going to feed on humans? I recoiled at the possibility. Humans had always loved and cared for me. The blood in my body seemed to congeal like the Jell-O that Tommy loved to snack on after school. *I don't want to harm humans.*

"You may have no choice. You are young. You might not be strong enough.

I sat back on my haunches in the fallen leaves that crunched under my weight. *I will fight against it at all costs.*

"Tomorrow night. We will test it then. First, we will return to the house. I have more to share with you." Slowly his red eyes changed to violet. His large, grotesque demon head, fangs and claws grew smaller, then back to a human head, teeth and hands. His twisted form returned to normal size, and the handsome Brogio smiled at me. He wiped the blood from his face with his arm, then turned back to his home. "Come, Snow Blood."

*****

We walked back to the house. Vines upon vines spanned for as far as I could see on both sides of the estate. Two marble dragons stood guard at the front gate. The lingering sweetness of the harvested grapes filled my nostrils. My senses kicked into overdrive. I could both smell and feel all the living creatures around me ... The rabbits and squirrels peering at us from the trees. The rotting corpses of dead birds. The traces of the humans who had been here earlier. The blood that ran through me exhilarated my body, yet somehow not quite enough. I longed for something ... more. Something I didn't understand. The need for human blood?

I tried to take my mind off what my body craved. I focused more sharply on my surroundings. The house and winery were layered with wooden beams and levels. The winery contained large, wrap-around windows so that those inside could see the outdoor beauty of Oregon. The beautiful mountains that my new master had called Mounts Hood and Jefferson rose in the distance.

My companion seemed to read my mind again. A prideful grin spread across his deceptively human face.

*****

We returned to the large rock fireplace in which a man could stand upright. The overhanging mahogany mantle held an ornate gold clock in its center. An inviting fire blazed and cast a soft glow around the room. Framed photographs of young people hung on the walls, and a small table next to Brogio's overstuffed chair held a re-filled wine canister and several wine glasses. A matching chair faced his on the other side of the fireplace. Brogio redressed and used a velvet towel hanging on one arm of the chair to wipe away the blood on his face and hands. He took a damp towel hanging on a small standing rack that had been placed in the room while we were gone, walked over to me and wiped down my body and face thoroughly. I wanted to resist, but the vigorous massage felt good. When he hung the towel back on the rack, it was covered in blood. He poured himself another glass of red wine.

I walked over to sit by his chair. So many questions were swirling around in my head about this vampire thing. But the sight of red wine brought me back to the subject of blood. I sat in shock at what I had just experienced. I asked the first question that sprang to mind. *So, Brogio, If you keep yourself alive with blood, why do you drink so much wine? And why sit next to a fire that you can't feel?*

"Just because I like it, I guess. The wine does nothing to me. But after all, I am a vintner. I love the taste of wine, especially red wine. And, I like to look at the fire. I enjoy the smell of burning wood."

Then, why did I not enjoy the taste of the meat you gave me earlier? It's something I've always loved.

"You need time to adjust. Food will no longer be necessary for you. Your transformation will take place over time. We won't know until later what your tastes will be ... or your gifts." He stretched out in the same large chair. He twirled his glass and stared into it in deep thought.

"Snow Blood, I need to tell you something important."

I stared at him in anticipation.

"What I didn't tell you before is that I hit you with my car on purpose. I meant to do it."

Anger flooded over me, and I jumped to my feet, confused and growling. *Why?*

He let out a weary sigh. "Because I thought you were the panwere that has been stalking me." He jumped up and began to pace again. His steps were so frantic in both directions that I thought he might wear a hole in the floor.

Why was it stalking you? I asked.

"That's the question, my boy. I don't know. He's been after me for weeks." He ran his long hands through his shaggy blond hair and took another sip of his blood-red wine. "Earlier this evening, it tried to jump me in Newburg."

In Newburg? My humans and I live in Newburg. How far is it from here?

"Just 10 miles."

What happened?

"I out-maneuvered it, but I could sense it in the woods following my car. When I saw you crossing the road, I thought I had him trapped at last. My mistake. Unfortunately, you were too mutilated for me to save."

You could have saved my life?

"I can heal injuries with my blood. But you died before I could save you. Your back was broken. Your ribs had punctured your lungs, and the car tore open your belly. You bled out while I fought the panwere. My only alternative was to turn you at the moment of your death." He walked out of the room.

I sat there absorbing his words. How could this be true? I didn't have a mark on me.

When he returned, he brought me a saucer of blood. "It's from a human blood bag. A taste of what's to come."

I wanted to resist it, but it smelled of a sweetness I never knew existed. I sat staring at it like an addict waiting for his next fix. When I could hold back no longer, I devoured it, and every hair on my body stood on end. A fire rushed through me like nothing I had ever felt, and I rolled over in ecstasy. I had transcended normal consciousness, but his words invaded my brain.

"Still think you will be able to resist?" He mocked me, but his words angered me, not at him but at myself.

Perhaps instead of killing humans I can get this blood elsewhere?

"We shall see. There's a possibility. We'll explore it tomorrow, and it might be more to our advantage."

Why didn't you let me die on the road?

"A fair question. I suppose after the actual panwere attacked me, and after I killed it, I saw you lying there dying. I wanted to save you. I meant you no harm. This was the only way. I've been alone with my own thoughts for too long."

I cared little for his loneliness. I could only think of my pack and my love for them. I came to them from my mother's teat. My Alpha and their little one had been all I have ever known. When I was still new to them, James taught me how to search for Tommy by sniffing his clothes. Then, Tommy would hide, and James would tell me to find him. James thought it great fun and would be good in case Tommy ever got lost in the woods. Our lives were filled with games and eating food that James and Tommy would hand me under the table when Jeanne wasn't looking! I tried to remember how long I had been with them. I had heard my Alpha tell someone not too long ago that I am four years old. Brogio said I wouldn't age. *So, I will be four years old forever?* I asked aloud in my head.

His words again crept into my brain. "You can't return. Your humans would be your first victims. I know you don't want that on your conscience."

I could never harm my humans. I didn't trust this man-demon. Why didn't he give me a choice about dying or enduring this living death? Was Brogio as selfish as he seemed? Was I to be his latest plaything? His experiment? Assuming that he was telling me the truth about all that happened until now, I was both enraged and grateful that he had provided me this imitation of life.

His mocking smile and piercing stare jolted me. *Can you hear everything that I think?*

"I can't hear you when I'm resting, or if one of the gods blocks me. Otherwise, I hear your every thought." His sneer widened.

One of the gods?

"Ah, that's a story for another time."

Another time? So what if I want to rip out your throat before "another time"?

"I really wouldn't blame you. But I am stronger, and you need me now. Perhaps you should wait and see the kind of power I hold before you get aggressive with me."

What choice do I have but to stay here ... with you ... now?

*****

Brogio slept the deep sleep of the Kindred in a wine cask next to me. A similar one awaited me. It contained a thick, comfortable pad. Who did it or how it was done was unknown to me. After he had made sure I was situated, Brogio had closed the container just before sunrise. I waited restlessly for slumber to take me as he had predicted. Time passed, and still I lay wide awake, my tail wagging and my tongue hanging out. I hadn't taken to daytime napping. I usually slept just after my nightly forage, hunting for prey, and always next to my James.

My life had been one of constant familiarity. Up early as the little one dressed for what they called "school". I always helped Tommy eat his breakfast, and had mine too. Nothing but good chow mixed with leftover scraps of chicken or beef for me. Then, off to take the boy to catch what he called his "bus" that took him away, but always brought him back hours later.

Every day, James went to a place filled with shelves and items like nails, hammers and drills. He always took me with him. People would come to him for the items, and that seemed to make James happy. But I would scoot out early in time to meet Tommy's bus in the afternoons ... just to ensure his safety. Then, we'd play ball until Jeanne would yell at him to "come in and do your homework." I'd trot back to James, always in time to wait for him to go home.

Once, a man who often visited what James called "the store" introduced himself as Anson, a "dog trainer." He commented on my looks, and said I could be a show dog. "He's a big husky, but that snow white fur, blue eyes, and great confirmation make him a perfect specimen," the man claimed. "You should let me take him and train with him for a while."

I didn't know the meaning of a specimen, but I understood that he thought I was good-looking and strutted around the store like one of those dogs on the shows Tommy watched on the flickering box they all called "television."

I stood looking up at both of them at the counter when James laughed. "My wife and son would have my head, Anson. That dog means more to them than anything. Me too, if truth be told."

I sighed at my memories and tried again to fall asleep. Finally, out of boredom, I fitfully dozed, only to repeatedly awake and wait for long periods of time for sleep to overtake me again. This wasn't what Brogio had said it would be. Finally, after completely giving my front legs a good grooming, and what seemed a very long time, I dozed off. Only this time, I was soon startled awake by the soft sound of glass breaking.

The hackles on the back of my neck stood on end. I smelled danger. What if someone meant us harm? Pushing aside my fear, I clawed at the container door and quickly nudged it open with my newfound strength.

Complete darkness shrouded the room, but I could see well with my keen senses.

I made my way to the door of the wine storage room that housed our resting places. Again, a simple nudge pushed it aside, but I cautiously shut it behind me to protect Brogio.

I could both smell and see that the sun would be setting soon. I crept up the stairs toward the sound of voices to investigate. I stopped short of the small strands of waning light that broke across the floor above the wine storage room where Brogio slept.

The voices of two men whispering reached my keen hearing. The acrid smell of wine offended my nostrils.

"Shut up, you fool. Stop trying to take bottles of wine. We don't have much time. The sun's going down!"

"Well, Smart Mouth, why did you wait so late? We shoulda come earlier."

I could hear the sound of glass bottles being set on the floor. Then, the pungent smell of unwashed bodies mingled with sweat and a faint hint of fear assaulted my nose.

"Because, you idiot, I had to make sure all the workers were gone. We gotta stake this sucker and get outta here so we can claim the money."

The hair on my back stood on end. They were going to put a stake in Brogio! I could not survive without him. Like it or not, he was my Alpha now … my pack master. I had to protect him.

"First, we gotta find 'em. Did the guy who hired us tell you where this thing sleeps?"

"Naw, but he thinks somewhere in the wine storage area. Be careful, fool, we was told this thing is dangerous when the sun goes down."

Sunlight slowly spread across the floor, and I backed away from it, afraid I would catch on fire. I had to help Brogio. He had been kind to me, tried to help me. Or at least that is what he had told me. I had to do the same. I stood indecisively for a few minutes, unsure exactly what to do.

A soft, oily voice crept into my mind. "Go ahead. You will be protected."

Startled, I turned around, looking in every direction for another intruder. No one appeared.

"Go on." The woman's voice tingled through my brain. Again, my eyes sliced through the dark corners of the room to discover no one.

I tentatively placed the end of a paw in the sun's path expecting to be scorched. Nothing. I could hear the men moving toward me. Another few inches of paw. Nothing. I put my head in the light. It caressed my fur – nothing else. The intruders' voices were closer. Can I ... but I'll catch on fire ... I have to help him ... don't want to burn to death and evaporate! I need him to live! I know nothing about how to be a vampire. Oh, shit! I stepped out into the light. I'm not on fire!

The ghostly female voice whispered in my mind. "You will repay me for this favor, Snow."

The men surprised me, signaling my inbred response to protect myself. All other thought dissolved. I crouched and growled out of fear. An old reflex. But, I began to change. The men appeared to grow smaller. My fangs extended, and I felt my entire body grow larger. The men watched me in horror and began to scream.

EPISODE TWO
Discovery

"**M**y God, it's a devil hound!"

The intruders in the wine cellar turned to run, but I sprang. A claw to the hamstring of the smaller man knocked him down. I almost felt guilty to knock down what would be considered the "runt of the litter" in dog terms.

The alpha of the two-man pack turned to defend his littermate. Shielding the smaller one, he reached for a long wooden stake, swung it with all his might, and slammed the blunt end against my back. Flipping it in his hand, he then stabbed at me with the sharp end repeatedly. Slow human. I simply outran the weapon, then leaped over him.

I came to a skidding stop on the cold concrete floor of the wine storage room, crouched again, and growled.

The fallen man cried out, "Jake, look at its eyes. It's a demon! Run!" Hurriedly, he lunged up the steps, taking three at a time in his frantic haste to escape.

The bigger man approached, again stabbing at me unsuccessfully with the sharp end of the stake. Next, he grabbed a bottle of wine from one of the overhead racks and swung it in my general direction. He must have thought he was the brains of the operation! No matter, I managed to duck each of his feeble efforts to injure me with his makeshift weapon.

I could hear his heart pumping blood through his body. Human blood. I suddenly wanted his blood above all else. The desire to kill him for it consumed me. The beast inside took control. I backed up, almost an inch away from a wall full of bottled wine, to draw him closer, and then I leaped onto his chest and took him down to the floor. He dropped the sharp stake, and the wine bottle shattered on the hard floor. He screamed as my teeth sank into his throat releasing the sweet nectar of the gods into my mouth. It ignited a fire within me and sent me into a frenzy to drain every drop of it. My victim's screams echoed throughout the cellar. His efforts to beat me with his hands atop my head had little effect. I sank my fangs deeper into his throat, sucking at his throbbing artery until Brogio's voice slammed into my brain.

"Snow Blood, no! Let him go!"

I could feel his will pulling at me. The more nectar I gulped down, the more painful the pull. The pain stripped my will, and I obeyed. I released my prey. The blood running down his neck teased me cruelly.

Brogio snatched the bleeding man, gripped his bloody throat, and hung him high in the air with one hand. The witless victim kicked to be free. Brogio dropped him to the concrete floor. "Who sent you here? Tell me now!" Brogio loomed over the cowering thief like a vulture ready to rip apart its prey.

The man began to speak. "It ... it was ..." His shrill scream engulfed the air. Foam bubbled from his mouth. His body twisted and contorted into great spasms, then silence.

"What the ..." Brogio bent over the man. "He's dead. How can that be? You didn't drain him."

I circled the dead man, sniffing. He smelled of death like the animals I had discovered in the forest during my nightly patrol at home. Their remains were the leavings of the predators who had preyed upon them. I wanted to finish devouring his blood, but the smell of him repulsed me. At the same time, guilt spread over me like a heavy blanket. I had never killer another before. I hadn't meant to kill him. I was only trying to protect Brogio. Something within me overpowered my ability to reason. I whined and walked to a corner and sat down. My body changed, until, without trying, I felt normal again.

"Damn it," Brogio clenched his fists.

He was here to stake you. He wanted to rob you of your wine and kill you as you slept.

"Yes, I figured as much. So my stalker hasn't given up." He sat down next to me and leaned back against a wooden column. "How did you intercept him so quickly?"

Still etched with guilt, I stretched out beside him. The euphoria of feeding on human blood spread through me, washing away my guilt. *The way they talked. Someone sent them for you. One got away. He ran up the stairs and fled.*

"Another accompanied him?" Brogio leapt to his feet, then vanished before my eyes, his racing footsteps sounding against the steps of the cellar.

Repulsed by the reek of death, and eager to help catch the other intruder, I sprinted up the cellar stairs and out the door, across the front lawn.

When I finally caught up to Brogio's scent at the opening of the forest, he had already split the man's neck open with his razor fangs and helped himself to dinner. I slunk behind him as he carried the half-dead thief back to the wine cellar. I followed him down the stairs as he dragged the man to the corner of the room, then threw him down on the cold concrete floor next to the lifeless, shriveled hulk of his accomplice.

What happened? I asked in my mind.

"He didn't know who hired them." Brogio pointed to my victim. "Yellow shirt had the contact and got hired. He brought the smaller one along to help him."

I watched the slowing pulse of Brogio's victim, could feel myself changing into the demon who had attacked the intruders.

"Yes, I know. You are still hungry for blood. I fed off him but left you enough to quench your thirst." Brogio pointed to the open wound on the man's neck.

Sheer terror engulfed the runt's eyes as I morphed into the raging beast. I fell on him and sank my fangs into the soft, wet flesh of his vulnerable neck. Blood! I drew deeply. He pounded me with his fists to no avail. As my jaws locked, he screamed like a demented soul, foam dripping from his mouth, shudders racking his body. He began to convulse. I reluctantly backed away, and Brogio and I both watched him try to rise and then collapse in the corner.

Brogio walked back to our victim, lifted his wrist, and felt his pulse, then turned to me with eyebrows raised. "He's dead. That's the second one in a row that you haven't drained that died. How peculiar."

I transformed back into my normal body then cocked my head at him. *I only bit him and drank a little of his blood. Same as the other.*

"And yet they both died instantly." He sat down next to a wine cask and withdrew into thought.

I stretched out on the cool concrete floor and yielded to the euphoria. My victims' blood surged through every part of me. How could so little blood have such a profound effect on me?

Brogio invaded my thoughts. "It's almost as if they had rabies. I've seen humans die with rabies before ... very similar." He stood, walked over to me, and knelt. "Bizarre. That must be one of your detriments." He stood and mumbled something about getting rid of the bodies. "Go to the house and wait."

I sat in the den next to the fireplace and wished I could feel its warmth. I couldn't get the other ghostly voice out of my head. The one that earlier encouraged me to run through the sunlight. It felt like oil sliding on water, soft but everywhere. The words sent shivers through me. Repay the favor? I hadn't asked for anything. So why did I owe for it?

The front door to the house swung open. Brogio returned from disposing of our victims. Dry blood covered his black sweater and spattered on his face and hands. His voice sliced through my thoughts.

"The voice you question – most likely Artemis. She is forever a frienemy. She's up to something, I suppose." Brogio sat down in his favorite chair next to the fireplace.

A *"frienemy"*? I didn't know what he meant.

"Artemis pretends to be my friend when it pleases her." Brogio picked at the blood on his sweater. "But, she's a god, and they all play games. They delight in the misery of others."

A god? Like the one Tommy says his prayers to at night?

Brogio rubbed his hands over his face like he was trying to think of the best way to explain to me. "No, not The God. A god. Immortal beings that play with humans and other creatures to amuse themselves."

They really exist? James used to read Tommy stories about gods in ancient times. I always listened too. I shifted on my haunches. This piqued my interest.

"Yes, they really exist. Just like vampires, werewolves, monsters and all the other creatures that humans want to believe are myths." Brogio stood and stretched.

Does she want to use me against you? Is it a game? I thought.

"Not sure yet ... I need to figure out who is stalking me, what he, or she, wants." He waved for me to follow him up the stairs.

We entered a large bedroom decorated with textured, soft materials. My human pack had never known such riches. I walked to the huge canopy bed covered with exotic mauve and gold colors. I could see them ... all my senses – sight, sound, taste, feel – were heightened. I sniffed the bed.

"Ah, so you like my mahogany bed?"

I barked once in approval.

"Great. Well, stay off it. I don't need to find dog hairs when I'm entertaining ladies." Brogio laughed and strolled over to a large closet where he selected another black sweater that covered his neck and black pants. He pulled clean underwear from a nearby large mahogany chest that matched his bed. He stepped into a large sunken shower made of marble and glass in the adjoining bathroom and washed himself thoroughly, especially scrubbing away the blood from his face and hands, before toweling off and stepping into clean clothes.

I took that moment to assess him. He reminded me of one of those handsome movie stars that Tommy's mother

Jeanne loved to watch on the large-screen "television" at home. His chiseled face, strong muscular physique and long pale blond hair would have made her sigh, as she often did while watching her favorite actors.

"I have a wine tasting in a few days. Let's go into Newburg to arrange the food for the event." He motioned for me to follow.

But won't I be recognized? People, even my humans, might see me. I gazed up at him questioning his logic.

"You'll stay in the car. It has tinted windows. No one will see you." He headed down the stairs and through the door to the right. It connected to the place he kept his cars. I obeyed and followed, but the hungering thirst returned. I whimpered.

"Don't worry. I'll make a visit to the hospital blood bank on the way home." He turned to me and opened the passenger door. "Don't want you trying to sustain yourself the normal way. After what we just experienced, a trail of dead bodies will surely lead back to us."

Will I always be hungry like this? I wondered how I could keep myself fed without eating blood all the time. My stomach knotted with my hunger.

"No. It's part of the transformation process. You will learn in time to curb your cravings." He rubbed my head with his hand and gave me a sympathetic look.

Suddenly, I was having second thoughts about Brogio. Perhaps he wasn't so bad after all. Even if he did ram me with his car and turn me into some bloodthirsty vampire dog.

We made the 10-minute drive into Newburg, and he went in to a familiar catering company. It was called Someone's In the Kitchen. The shop stood out on the street with its bright blue awning, and pies and cakes in the front window. It was a place James used to take me. I remembered sitting outside while he went in to get meat and cheese platters for parties. All those delicious turkey rolls he brought home used to make my mouth water. But now the thought of them repulsed me, which felt so odd, even troubling.

Brogio exited the car. I jumped into the backseat just to make sure I wouldn't be seen. I watched him enter the store. A big glass door closed slowly behind him. And just as I settled in, I caught a whiff of a familiar scent coming from outside the car. I watched carefully as a man walked down the street in the dark. He carried a large rolled-up poster. His head was down, but the body was familiar. He drew nearer, and I recognized my James. The rush of love and blood lust battled within me. His blood seemed to call to me. Through the confines of the car, the sweet smell of the liquid coursing through his veins lingered in my mind. He was prey. His nectar would be mine. No! He isn't prey! I love him. I can't ever, ever harm him!

I struggled as the drool gathered in my mouth and dropped in great globs on the leather seat. But, I wanted him! I needed to follow him into the small store and rip his throat open, sucking the life force from him! Or, did I just want to lick his face and express my unconditional love for him? I was startled at these conflicting emotions. Brogio was right. I couldn't be trusted with my own humans again. The sadness of this stung me hard.

My paws grew. The car would be too small for my hulking form if I transformed.

I closed my eyes and shook my head, fighting the transformation. At the same time, I envisioned throwing my body against the car window, smashing it, and diving head-first into the storefront window. There would be more than just my human to devour ... the people that worked in the store, other customers. My body began to grow ... I was losing all control.

Brogio's ability to read my mind was the only thing that could prevent a massacre. "No, Snow Blood." His voice rang in my head. "Suppress your desire. This is your human. He wants to post a sign offering a reward for anyone finding you. He misses you. So does the little boy. Remember what I told you?"

He was right! James, my old Alpha. I would kill my beloved pack leader. I had become a monster. I flattened my ears in sorrow and buried my head into the backseat, thinking of easier days. Tommy would be begging his mother for a bedtime cookie, and he would share a corner of it with me when she wasn't looking. How I missed this loving affection.

The car door opened, and Brogio rubbed my snout playfully, artfully ignoring my near disaster. "The catering order is all set. My assistants will pick it up tomorrow. Now to the blood bank. I'll get enough to last you for a while.

And, as time goes by, I will teach you how to suppress your urges more easily."

Perhaps I will learn to live off the animals of your forest for my survival?

"Perhaps." He gave me a grimace. "But for now, the Providence Newberg Medical Center is always good for a gourmet meal."

Brogio scored a very large container of human blood bags as promised. The delicacies hardly made it to the floor. I gorged on several units, one bag after another as he drove home. My ears wiggled, "delicacies." I hadn't known the word before but understood it now. How?

The human blood coursed through my veins. The rush of it throughout my body almost knocked me unconscious. I had never experienced anything to which I could compare it.

As we drew near Brogio's estate, unbridled strength and the need to run free whispered promises from the woods just beyond the darkest hours of night.

"Shall we supplement the feast?" Brogio smiled.

He opened the door to the sound of crickets, the mating call of owls, and random screeches of creatures I could potentially eat. My paws landed on dirt. The sounds of night stilled. They knew I was free to chase, catch, and devour. Fear comes in many forms, but the smell of fear is always the same. Vampire or not, I knew the smell of weakness.

A predator broke the stillness first. A stalky cat, too big to be in the care of humans, ran down a path between a pair of oak trees. I snared it without transforming into a demon this time. Grabbing it by the neck, I shook it until it went limp then punctured its jugular as Brogio had shown me. The cat's blood tasted of too much fur, mixed in with sweet ecstasy.

I quickly learned that vampires have superhuman strength. The taking of life and blood is second nature to us. We were created to feed on the blood of others, and it is no more difficult than humans sitting down to a meal.

Brogio kneeled beside me, pretending as though he would take my prize. My warning growl displeased him.

"The carcass needs to be disposed of. I will do it."

I gnashed at the limp neck squeezing the last droplets of blood.

Brogio pressed his lips together. I felt a pull on my will, and then it stopped.

"There's a homeless man in a nasty old raincoat sleeping down by the water. I was going to get my dinner and take care of your leftovers at the same time."

I surrendered the carcass and sauntered behind him. We headed through a clearing in the woods, down a path to the river. Belly-full of blood and no interest in feeding further, my sense of alertness grew. If something wanted Brogio dead, I needed to be on guard. My survival depended upon my new Alpha staying alive.

Suddenly, Brogio vanished. There in one moment and then gone. Fresh blood in my stomach gave me renewed purpose. Our mind connection kept me from panicking. He ran fast. Nose to the ground, I picked up his scent of cologne.

Trees blurred my vision. His cologne created a beacon for anyone who wanted to find him. Any creature with a strong sense of smell would easily track him. I commanded my legs to stretch further, my strides to become longer.

I willed conversation with him. *Stop wearing that cologne.*

His laughter filled my head. "You think I should change it?"

I think you should stop wearing any stink spray.

"But the ladies like it."

It's like a beacon for predators!

"And if they follow it, they will be met with death."

I growled, my frustration growing. He was very set in his ways.

At the end of the dirt path, I arrived at the river and stopped near the last trees before water's edge. I found Brogio on top of a reeking garbage bag of a man near the water. He smelled of garlic and dead fish. He wore an old raincoat that was smeared with dirt, grease and something that looked like the leavings of multiple meals from a trash can. How could Brogio stand to be near him, let alone feed

39

off him? Long sucking noises brought drool to my mouth, watering for a taste even from this stinking pile of prey.

My new Alpha cradled his victim in his arms. The beating of his heart slowed and then stilled. When Brogio finished, he gently licked the wounds and laid the man's head against his bedroll.

"*Eterno riposo, concedere a loro, o Signore, e lasciare che perpetua risplenda ad essi la luce Maggio le anime dei fedeli defunti attraverso il ricordo di Dio, riposa in pace, AMEN.*"

It sounded mournful. I wondered why.

Reading my mind, he answered. "It is the Italian lament for the dead. After a millennium of taking human life, I still honor what they give to me."

The gentleness of his words surprised me. I could add compassion to his small, but growing list of attributes.

Suddenly, I smelled danger. Something very large moved fast toward us. *Brogio, you are being stalked! Watch out!*

The creature attacked him in the middle of my mental warning. It had the head and body of a lion. Another head ... something that looked like a goat head growing out of its back. On the other end, it possessed a snake-like tail, which slammed Brogio's body against a tree trunk, knocking him to the ground. The goat head spat a ball of fire in the direction where Brogio had fallen. The flames just missed singeing his long blond hair.

The recent blood I'd consumed rushed through my body and transformed me into my oversized self. I was leaning back on my hind legs, ready to leap. That's when Brogio's thoughts stopped me. "Wait. Stay where you are!"

Brogio changed before my eyes. He morphed into a broad body with a long tail. His clothes ripped and fell around him. Plate-like scales the color of shiny bronze covered his body. His legs changed to short limbs with five closely-mounted digits and long claws on each foot. Strange wings and a row of tendrils grew out of his back. Tiny nostrils appeared on either side of what looked like a snout, from which a single horn emerged. Two feelers extended backwards from his forehead. His ears dissolved into two tiny holes, and his chin grew to a point. Large eyes the color of dying embers smoldered as he assessed his challenger. He exchanged streams of fire with the lion-goat creature. The surrounding trees ignited, and the fire spread quickly. Brogio shouted to me in a commanding voice. "Snow, head for home, now!"

I stood my ground under the fire-filled trees next to the lake, fascinated as the two creatures circled each other. They literally breathed fire at each other. Long streams of scalding flames encircled both of them. The dragon-like creature that Brogio had become now backed his opponent further into the woods. Suddenly the attacking beast used its lion-like body to leap at my master. Brogio quickly evaded the beast and blew more streams of fire around his opponent.

The Brogio-dragon creature focused a wild-eyed stare on me, and I heard the words: "Go. Now!" I felt Brogio's fear, not for his own life, but for my safety.

A wall of flame blocked my view, and I backed away and ran deeper into the woods, far from the fire.

The screams of the two creatures echoed throughout the forest. Small animals and birds scampered for cover. The air stank of thick smoke. A final roar was followed by silence, except for the crackling of the trees still burning. Heavy footsteps crashed through the woods. I sped up, running as fast as my vampire legs would carry me. The trees became a blur. The dragon ran past me, changing as it did into the naked vampire. Fire truck sirens wailed in the distance.

That thing could have killed you! I shouted in my head.

"Perhaps, but it did not succeed. The sirens forced it to flee." He slowed down as we neared his estate. "You go ahead, Snow Blood. I need some time to collect my thoughts."

I agreed, thinking I would hear his thoughts.

His laughter shook the trees. "You'll never know what you can and can't hear. Go back to the house. I need time."

I turned and slunk away in the direction of the vineyard. Brogio might try to stop me from hearing his thoughts, but if I concentrated, I guessed that I might be able to hear something. More laughter echoed after me. As hard as I tried, I couldn't hear him. My worry for his safety had become sincere at this point. I halted and turned away from going to the house. Instead, I crept back to find him.

I maneuvered my way back to the last place I'd seen him. Even in my formidable size, I did my best not to make any noise. I couldn't see him, but his scent lingered. My nose twitched, sorting out the different aromas of a wounded creature, burnt wood, an "otherness" smell, and the musk of Brogio's cologne. My senses clasped onto the one I wanted, and I followed it. It led away from the burning trees. Being the hunter that I am, my paws tread lightly on leaves and branches on the ground. During this time of year, trees shed more than I ever did.

I stopped in a tree-lined area that left me a clear view of the glowing moon before me. Ridiculous as it seemed, I actually felt the moonlight before I saw it. Nothing within a twenty-meter radius escaped the blue tinges of light. Brogio, still in his human form, stood naked in the far reaches of a circle surrounding a woman. She was, in a plain word, beautiful. Not the kind of beautiful like my human Alpha's mate, Jeanne. A less tangible beauty. One could call it strength, or confidence, but I could not look away. Light flowed around her, as mist would cling to water. It lingered near her body, like it wanted to touch her but couldn't. Perhaps she warded it off? Even the trees bowed to her beauty and command. A rabbit sitting at the edge of her light stared at her like it knew her. It revered her.

"Why, Artemis?" Brogio spoke with a tone of utter defeat and anger. The sound of his words made my heart ache.

Artemis was the one Brogio called his "frienemy."

A sound of chimes physically collided with the mist surrounding who I perceived to be the god Brogio warned against. Swirls of light and voice danced in slow spiral. "You do not appreciate my gift?"

"Gift?" Brogio snorted in disgust. "You call a Chimera, a panwere, and two thugs a gift?"

"Those are not my gift to you." Mist and sound danced once more. "I meant the gift you stole from me."

"What could I have possibly stolen?" Brogio looked straight at me.

I tucked my tail and hid behind a tree.

"Plenty." Artemis swept her hand over the forest. She too seemed to see right through the tree I hid behind. "You know, my bow never found its way back to me."

"But, I meant to save my soul! You know the deal Hades made with me ... the silver bow ... if I didn't give it to him, I would have had to live in hell forever and never see my love again." Brogio sighed. "Just like all of you, he's a trickster. I've paid the price."

"I dare to think you haven't. Or not enough."

"Not enough? The curse of silver burning my skin for stealing your bow? Turning me into this thing? This thing that's supposed to be a greater hunter ... draining the blood of humans and beasts to live in immortality? For what? To worship only you? I could have done it all. But you took her away from me. That wasn't enough?"

44

I lay trembling behind the tree. Brogio's words shocked me. Did this Artemis woman make Brogio a vampire?

"Selene is still yours." Artemis' light swirled brighter around her.

Despite my trembling, my ears remained glued to their exchange. This information about Brogio fascinated me. But who is Selene?

Brogio spread his arms wide. "And yet my love is not here with me. On the night you promised me her immortality if I would take her blood, you stole her away from me and made her part of the moonlight!"

"What more could you want? You still feel her during the moon's height of power."

"Not for some time have I felt her presence. But that gift didn't turn out to be so much as a gift than a curse!"

"Yet you still take yourself in hand during the full moon. Do you think that's how you'll receive children from her? I told you, its blood, not semen that will give you children."

Flustered, Brogio raised both arms and yelled, "Children you call them?"

"This wouldn't have happened if you'd stayed in Florence!" Artemis swirled again.

"Then I wouldn't have met Selene!"

"That is the point."

"What point!" Brogio's agitation increased. "Explain yourself to me."

I could feel myself hanging on their every word. But their words confused me. Blood would give him children? Did she mean vampires?

The mist swirled around the one Brogio called Artemis. "You enticed the sister of the Oracle! A maiden of my brother's temple! Apollo longed for the virgin Selene in his temple. He tried to win her for himself until *you* appeared."

"Damn you, Artemis! You know Selene and I fell in love, were to be married, and return to Italy."

Artemis swirled a little closer to Brogio. I could feel her eyes on me, and I cowered in the darkness.

"Selene infatuated Apollo, you fool. Still does! You were such an adventurer that you thought you could go into his temple and violate his rights! Why do you think his curse took the sunlight away from you?"

Her words jolted me. Selene is still alive? Apollo? I remembered James reading a story to Tommy and me about Apollo, the god of light, the son of Zeus. In the story, he had a twin sister named Artemis. And it was his job to drive the sun chariot across the sky each day. He took the sunlight away from Brogio?

Brogio clenched his fists in frustration. "Why, Artemis ... talk to me! Why are these creatures stalking me? Is it Apollo, or have I angered another God? What have I done?" He remained staring at her. "Why are you refusing to speak to me?"

The whispers quickly invaded my mind. They appeared to shut out any intrusion. Like oil, they slid through my brain, whispering secrets. You are championing Brogio now because he saved you. Yes, he is right. I am angry. He took you from me.

Brogio seemed unaware of the whispers in my head, so I answered. *Took me from you? But, I was dying. Take pity on him. He is lonely. He saved me to be his friend.*

The voice resonated throughout my skull, louder, irritated. *You were to be mine!*

Shocked, I questioned her. *To be yours? Why?*

Her silence made me try to reason with the glowing voice. *He mistook me for the panwere. He saved me. His guilt made him feel responsible for me. I can see the sadness in him. Can't you?*

A long silence, and then the whispers came in softer tones, almost caressing me.

I will let you stay with him for now. You are a worthy friend. The voice trailed off softly.

Wait! I begged. *How can I help Brogio overcome his sadness? Will my friendship be enough?*

Again, her cryptic answer came after a moment of silence.

Find the one who glows as bright as the moon. She will lift the sadness from his heart.

I felt the voice slip away.

I waited, hidden in the trees after the vision disappeared. I watched Brogio intently until he finally gave up hope for an answer to his plea. He stood and surveyed the landscape. He finally stepped back several feet closer to me and sighed. "I know you're there, Snow Blood. No need for hiding from me now."

But how did you ...

"You are my child now. I always know where you are ... what you are thinking." He turned to face me. "Did she talk to you? She has the ability to block me from you. Did she?"

Will you tell me more about the one called Selene?

His face softened at the sound of her name. He hesitated for a moment, appearing to struggle with himself. Without answering, he headed toward the house, and, like the good child, I followed. He picked up a red velvet robe from his large chair in front of the fire and wrapped it around his naked body. He tied the red belt, poured a glass of wine in a crystal glass, and sat down in his big chair.

My curiosity from the scene I just witnessed left me full of questions. I tried to organize them in my head and directed my thoughts to Brogio. *Are you okay? Did that strange monster that attacked you do you harm?*

"No, I'm fine. It will take something worse than that to take me down. Thanks for being concerned."

I wondered if the mention of the word "Selene" would take him down. I decided to avoid it. *What about that glowing woman? Is she the "frienemy"?*

"She is Artemis. My patron God." He gestured toward a large dog bed, covered with the same elegant fabric as in his bedroom. It had been placed just across from his chair near the fireplace while we were gone to town. Presumably for my comfort.

I walked to the bed and rubbed against the soft fabric. It felt silky smooth against my fur. *Like in the stories about Greek gods?*

He nodded his head in affirmation. "Yes, except they aren't just stories."

I decided to dive in head-first on my next question. Hard as I tried, I couldn't resist. *And Selene! Who is she?* I scratched at the bed, made several circles and plopped down on the soft cushion with my legs curled under me.

He twisted in his chair slightly and sipped his wine for a moment before answering.

"My mortal wife."

Alpha female? We have an Alpha female? Where is she?

Brogio shook his head. "Long since passed."

I don't understand. Isn't she a vampire like you?

"No." He whispered. "She was not immortal like me."

Another wave of sadness overwhelmed me. I knew instantly that it wasn't my sadness but Brogio's. In that moment, he let me feel what he felt. Then, cold tendrils of pure hate glided through my veins. The room dimmed. I felt myself growl. As fast as it came, the anger got snatched away from me like a toy being withdrawn. I didn't mind losing this particular bone. He was letting me know that tonight wasn't the night he would discuss Selene.

"Okay, Snow. Time to retire." Brogio leaped from his chair and motioned me to follow him to his rest.

I stood up from my new bed by the fireplace, wagging my tail. *But wait. I still have so many things to ask you about ...*

His voice silenced me. "I will speak of this no longer tonight. We have had quite an adventure. We need to get some rest."

I followed him out the front door as the first rays of the sun lit up the October morning. He headed into the winery and downward into his resting room.

"Tomorrow night, one of my other children will visit." He gave me a quick look of anticipation as he started to shut the wooden lid to his cask.

Other child? Who, who is it?

"Try to rest, Snow Blood. We both need it."

If only I could. But this cask you made for me ... there's a problem with that.

"What problem? Is the padding not sufficient?"

No, it's not that. But last night, when you put me in here, I couldn't sleep.

"What do you mean you couldn't sleep ... weren't you pulled into slumber?" He opened his cask door wider and stared at me, his eyes changing from purple to red, and slowly back again.

No. Not for a minute. And when I heard the noise above, the sound of the wine thieves, that's when I crept out. The sun streaked the sky. It didn't burn me.

He bolted out of his cask and rushed to my side, his glowing eyes wide as tennis balls. "So you can go about in the daylight?" He took hold of my face and peered into my eyes. "This must be one of your gifts!"

A voice inside my head ... a softer voice whispered, "Yes, a gift, a gift of daylight from ... Artemis ... A favor you will repay someday."

"Then, tomorrow," Brogio continued as if he heard nothing, "we'll move another bed near the door in here so that you can keep watch."

Brogio patted the top of my head, then turned and climbed back into his cask. He pulled the lid shut and was soon in a deep sleep.

I sought to try to find some rest if I could. I no longer felt his presence in my mind. I lay just inside the storage room door to guard against more intruders. My body felt weary from a lack of any true rest over the course of several nights. It wasn't long before I drifted off. But just as I began to close my eyes, one question kept repeating itself in my head. How will I find the one who glows as bright as the moon?

I awoke before the sun set. My head swirled with fragments of dreams. Creatures fleeing for their lives ...

slaughtering little Tommy, my human brother, before James' eyes ... a faceless woman who taunted me.

I jumped up, shook off sleep and pushed open the door to the hallway. The quiet stillness of the day's remainder slid behind the trees as I emerged outside. I watched as the last of the wine workers drove off while the sun set beyond the surrounding vineyard. A beautiful sight. Cool evening air crept through my nostrils. I breathed in the scent of a rabbit crunching on a leaf, and the Calico mousers who hawked a nest of mice. The smell of the sunset and the surrounding woods mingled with ... Brogio's infernal cologne. "Infernal?" How did I know that word? Was it possible that Brogio had somehow forced some of his knowledge into my mind?

Suddenly, his hand rested gently on my head. He must have snuck up behind me. "Good evening, Snow Blood. I trust you slept well?"

Well, better than last night in the cask. But I had terrible nightmares.

"Yes, to be expected. It's part of the transformation." He strode off toward the house, and I followed. "Come, let's prepare for Kane's visit."

Kane? Who is that? I trotted along beside him keeping up with his fast pace.

"He is my oldest son."

Your oldest son? Will you tell me about him?

"You will learn quickly enough that he is a prankster. And somewhat of a dandy in the way he dresses. But he has a decent heart if truth be told."

Is he your actual son by birth? Or did you make him a vampire?

Brogio opened the front door of the house and gave me a brief smile that reflected a good memory. "My first vampire child. Eons ago, Snow, in Italy."

Please tell me more about Kane.

Brogio, shrugged with a sigh. "I refused to make another vampire for a long time after I became one. Kane and I were friends. Always the adventurer, when he discovered what I was, he asked that I give him immortality. So, I did." He turned and strode off to the kitchen.

Wait. Why are you in such a hurry? I followed him as he instructed several of his wine makers to bring in a number of bottles of wine, along with what looked like large bags of blood.

"Because, Kane drinks a lot of wine, and the blood keeps him in one place long enough to visit with him. Did I tell you he's quite the lady's man as well? My son is a total stud!"

Kane arrived at the house just hours later. Brogio and I sat by the fire, he in his big chair, me on my bed, when the front door opened, and Kane yelled. The young man strolled in and uttered in a funny voice, "I'm home!"

His appearance startled me. He looked the complete opposite of Brogio. He stood a head shorter than his father.

53

He looked to be in his mid-twenties. Quite an elegant dresser, as Brogio had advertised. Almost flamboyant in a gold shirt and jacket, and black pants. A black scarf tucked into the opening of his shirt. Dark hair and eyes that sparkled with mischief. The devil seemed to run through his veins. He questioned my presence instantly to Brogio.

"A dog? You turned a dog? What in shit's name were you thinking?"

"That is not your concern. Only mine!" Brogio shot back. Despite his guarded tone of voice, I could see by the hint of a smile on his face that Kane amused Brogio.

"So, dog, what do you bring to the table?" Kane leaned down and stared into my eyes.

I growled a deep-throated warning for him to back off, and he did so, laughing.

They sat down together next to the fire and shared wine, while I cocked my head, sat on my elegant bed next to Brogio's chair, and listened to their banter.

"So, *Dad*, how's it going with all those strange attacks? Have you figured out who's hunting you?"

"Not yet," Brogio answered in a clipped voice. "I'll let you know when I do."

Kane stared at me above his wine glass. "Lonely are we?" He pointed in my direction. "Brogio, I'm wondering if maybe I should visit more often? Do you actually talk to this furry creature?"

"Just as I have with you, Kane, we have a mind connection." Brogio took a sip of his wine and stretched out his legs.

Kane leaned forward in his chair. "Why do you need him? Are my bi-annual visits not enough?

I let out a low growl, and Brogio laughed. "There's you answer!"

Kane ignored Brogio's mock and continued. "I mean, it's not like you don't have plenty of ladies to keep you company! That's so convenient ... first you tumble them, then you have them for dinner!" Kane threw his head back and let out an infectious laugh that even had Brogio smiling.

Brogio sipped his wine and stared at his son.

Kane stared back and smiled. "At least it's a better deal than you had with Selene."

Brogio shifted uncomfortably in his chair and shot a warning glare at Kane.

Kane ignored him and leaned toward me. "Did our father tell you his story yet? He is the first of us, after all."

"Shut up, Kane!" Brogio slammed his wine glass down on the table, shattering it and throwing its contents everywhere.

Startled, I leaped to my feet, growling. One of Brogio's assistants quickly entered to sweep up the shards of glass. I got the feeling this was an everyday occurrence when Kane visited. I watched with curiosity as the silent assistant efficiently swept everything away and left the room, never being acknowledged by either vampire.

"Come on, father! I mean, what a waste ... giving up your humanity. And for what? You couldn't even have Selene like you should have!"

I sat up in anticipation. Perhaps this Kane would give me some of the answers to my endless list of questions.

"Yes, it's the aged old chicken-and-egg argument! He never wants anyone to know he's the original!" Kane stretched out his legs and yawned. "It's all in *The Vampire Bible*. He's really old! Ancient." He chuckled as his words trailed off.

A slow, cold anger crept into the pit of my stomach, but the poison that intruded into my gut was not my own.

Brogio sprang from his chair and lifted Kane by the throat! "By Hades, that's enough!" He threw Kane back in the chair and stomped off and out the front door. Kane's laughter followed him, as did I.

I sprinted out the door and into the woods after my sire. I tried to track him for a while with no luck. Hunger began to consume me, so while in the woods, why not feed? Blood lust embraced me just as I spied a large stag that sprinted away the moment it heard me coming. I gave chase, but before I could overtake the deer, a black beast charged through the trees and stepped in front of me, snatching my prey. With quick precision, the beast slit the deer's throat and sucked it dry in front of me. The hulking beast turned to me, blood dripping from its fangs, and an odd smile spread across its homely face. Its snout, horns and fangs quickly dissolved into the human face and naked body of Kane, who threw his head back and let out his obnoxious laugh. He wants to best me!

Frustrated, I leaped around Kane and buried my nose to the ground, picking up the musky scent of a small boar. Kane's laughter filled my ears. He intrigued and infuriated me at once. But why? He actually had done nothing other than goad Brogio and me. Could some kind of sibling rivalry be to blame? Nonsense! I barely knew Kane.

I blocked out Kane's laughter and tracked down the boar, hiding in the thicket near the river. I pounced on its back, knocking it to the ground, sideways. Then with one mighty swipe, I tore open its jugular, and feasted on its squirting blood as its body flopped about fighting against me. Eventually, the animal lay peacefully still. I leaped to my feet and turned back in the direction of the estate.

Kane joined me in my homeward sprint. "Curious are you, dog? Me too. After he turned me, I heckled him until I got more information out of him. Maybe if you're nice, I'll tell you." He moved toward the house and entered it.

Instead of following Kane, I hurriedly circled the house several times, looking for Brogio, hoping to console him. There was no sign or scent of him anywhere in the area, I gave up the search and headed back inside the house.

A fully-dressed Kane sat in Brogio's big chair sipping a freshly poured glass of wine next to the fire in the den. I walked over and sat next to the fireplace, wishing I could feel its warmth.

"If you are looking for my father, you won't find him until he's calmed down. As usual, I've probably pushed him too far." Kane picked lint from his pants then examined the fingernails on his left hand.

My eyes begged him for some part of Brogio's story. Kane threw back his head and laughed. "You'd better learn to play poker better than you do, dog! What you want is written on your face."

I moved closer to stand by his chair and beseeched him with my eyes. My begging seemed to have worked.

"Okay. I've kept you in suspense long enough. I can never resist telling a good story!"

I sat back on my haunches and licked my chops.

"Brogio was human thousands of years ago, or so he tells me. Italian. An adventurer. He went to Delphi to have the Oracle read his fortune." Kane took another swallow of his wine, and the glint in his eye told me he did so to string out the information I so wanted to learn. "Some fortune. Something about a curse, the moon and blood. Pretty accurate I'd say."

I crept near and searched his face for deception.

"He stole her from Apollo ... Selene. They loved each other the moment they saw each other. She was a maiden in Apollo's temple. The god cursed him. The sunlight burns his skin. All our skin."

What happened with Selene? I asked in my head.

Nothing. No reply. He couldn't hear me. Instead, he got up to pour another glass of wine and gulped it down. He stood in front of the fire appearing to enjoy the warmth.

"These damn gods are always interfering with each other. Artemis took pity on our father. She made him immortal. Said he could be with Selene, and they had to worship only her. But, there was a catch. There's always a catch."

I cocked my head and stared at him with anticipation. What was it?

"A virgin goddess expects all her followers to remain chaste." He ran his hands through his dark hair. "In your lingo, dog, he couldn't ..."

"Silence, Kane!" Brogio stood in the doorway, still angry.

"Oh, come on, Brogio! Your pet should hear your story. He'll have to watch you mope around for eternity." As the last words slipped from his mouth, Kane began to choke. He fell to his knees, clutching his throat, and gasping for air.

Brogio leaped from the room to the front door, shedding his clothing and shoes. His body instantly transformed into a huge, screaming eagle. He pushed open the front door with his beak, stepped outside, and flew away. Meanwhile, Kane remained struggling to catch his breath on the floor.

I ran to the front yard and watched as the eagle/Brogio swirled and dive-bombed close to the earth, picking up mice and squirrels that scampered in a vain attempt to avoid his sharp talons. He devoured them in the air.

I shook my head in disbelief, finally sitting back to wait for the next revelation.

This tantrum abruptly ended when he landed in front of me, changed back into his naked human form, and ran into the field, screaming at the moon. "ARTEMIS! Answer me!" I followed. He swirled so fast that he almost became a tornado as his screams echoed across the field. "I knew you would deceive me … like always! You knew I couldn't refuse once Selene begged me to do it! I bit her neck … took her blood into my body!"

Artemis appeared in a shaft of light that illuminated the entire field. She shimmered there, her mouth slashed in a grimace. Her voice emphasized her anger. "Yes, the newly created vampires carry the blood of the two of you, together!"

"I didn't beg you for her to become a goddess!" Brogio seethed with anger. He raised his fists to the swirling image shrouded in moonlight. "I wanted to be with her, touch her, love her. Instead, you took her to be with you!"

Artemis swirled, making a tornado of her own. "You ingrate! Enough! I will hear no more! You earned your curses … live with them." She dissolved as a puff of smoke into the atmosphere.

Brogio stood there, empty and impotent, while Artemis dissolved back into the sky. Bloody tears ran down his face. He feebly attempted to wipe them away with one hand as he made the long walk back to the house. Once inside, he mounted the stairs to his bedroom.

I followed him to the stairs, but he shouted over his shoulder at me. "Stay, Snow. I need some time alone."

From what I had now discovered, it appeared that the gods had turned Brogio into a vampire and had stolen his wife from him. All very confusing.

I found Kane next to the fire. He straightened his clothes and poured another glass of wine. I wondered how he had been able to recover so quickly. Did all vampires have the ability to heal quickly from injury?

He glanced my way, and I padded up to him and peered into his eyes.

"No, I'm okay, dog. It's difficult to kill someone who's already dead. Just had my neck nearly crushed."

I whined and sat back on my haunches next to him hoping to get more information.

My wishes went unnoticed. He sighed. "Well, I guess I've done enough damage for one night!" His laugh dissolved into a fit of deep coughing.

My eyes pierced his, and I willed him to give me the last piece of the puzzle.

"I really need to go." He stood and swallowed his wine in a single gulp. "Our visits always end this way. We won't see him again tonight most likely." He placed his glass on the small table next to the chair and turned to me.

When will you return? I tried screaming the words in my head to make him hear me. It didn't work. Instead, I walked to him and beseeched him with my eyes to tell me the rest.

He gently patted me on the head. "I'll be back in a month or so to try and make amends. You can wait for the rest of it until then."

I growled and placed my body in front of the door to block his leaving. I bared my teeth and increased my growling. He was a powerful Kindred, but perhaps he wouldn't want to tangle with me tonight.

"Oh, for Hades' sake! All right! I'll tell you. I knew you'd want to know the rest!"

I wagged my tail feverishly, then leaned back on my hind legs.

Kane stood leaning against the doorpost, still rubbing his sore neck. "Artemis forced him to drink Selene's blood. It killed her mortal body. Their blood mixed together. It created eternal life for any who drank it. Artemis promised Selene would always be with him. She lied, as usual. Instead, she took Selene with her as part of the moonlight or wherever the hell she goes." He sighed. "Without Selene, Brogio has a hollow place in his heart and soul. He was a carefree adventurer until he met her. She was everything to him, and he has never recovered from losing her. Has no hope of ending his damnation and loneliness." He rubbed one hand over his eyes. "And, instead of the companionship I should offer, I heckle him like the scoundrel I am." He chuckled as he stepped around me and vanished out the door.

Brogio was the very first vampire? Had I just learned how vampires had been created? Was there more to this story? Did any of this have anything to do with Brogio's stalker? What could possibly happen next in this endless nightmare?

I went to my bed next to the fire and waited.

Brogio didn't return to the fire that night. Kane's unsettling visit unbalanced me. I imagined what it must have done for my new Alpha. I spent the rest of the night with my nose close to the ground, sometimes stalking prey, at other times just being a dog. I marked my territory in a wide circle around the estate. I rolled in rotten leaves and worms and the resting places of forest creatures, marking my territory. After all, I was still a dog, and that's what we like to do. As the sun rose, I reluctantly entered the resting room and lay on the bed Brogio had made for me next to the door. An uneasy sleep crept over me. I dreamed of vicious demons lurking in the woods.

"Egad, Snow Blood, you stink!" Brogio's voice shook me from a deep slumber.

I got to my feet and squinted up at Brogio. *What's wrong with the way I smell?*

"We're having a wine tasting here tonight, and you're covered with filth. You'll offend our guests. Come to the shower with me. Now!"

I followed him up the wine cellar's two landings of stairs, across the yard, and into the house. He pointed for me to go up the stairs, then waved for me to get into his sunken shower in the bathroom. I slunk into it as he removed his usual black turtle neck, pants, and shoes. He joined me and turned on the water, hosed me down and lathered me with sweet-smelling soap. I displayed my displeasure by slicking my ears back and growling as he rubbed me thoroughly. My bared teeth didn't deter him from his mission. The rub down felt good, but I suspected that the soap might present a problem. *I'm going to alert every creature in the woods, smelling like this!*

"Silence! I want you to stand guard outside the event tonight. There's no guessing what the gods will throw at me next!" He toweled me off, and I ran into his bedroom and rolled on the soft carpet, shaking the water from my fur.

Will others like Kane come to your party? I tried to rub up against the soft material on the large bed, but Brogio grabbed me by the back of my neck.

"Stay off the bed, dog!"

Well, will they? I imagined what Brogio would have been like as a carefree adventurer, kind-hearted, free-spirited. His endless loneliness had made him into an angry, closed-off creature.

He gave me a strange look, and I realized he had heard my thoughts.

"No, they won't." He pulled on more black clothing. This time, the material more formal. A black shirt and pants with a silver belt and black shoes and socks. He topped if off with a black jacket that appeared to made from a heavy brocade.

Where are the others that you have made?

"Everywhere. But nowhere near here. Enough questions." He sighed and ran a brush through his long, blond hair.

I had to admit we made a handsome pair ... the tall man with pale hair and violet eyes, and the blue-eyed, white, oversized dog at his side.

"Snow Blood, we have a big night ahead. I've had enough of the past for now."

Somehow, I had a premonition that this night would be full of the past for Brogio as the oily voice crept into my mind.

Soon.

EPISODE THREE
Selene

The night air brought an aroma of the dark surrounding forest. Owls beckoned to me: "Catch me if you can." A squirrel scurried up a tree to dine on a tasty nut it had found on the earthen floor. A snake curled around a branch ready to devour a tree mouse. My sole amusement as I sat guard for what seemed eternity outside the wine tasting. The moon peaked high in the sky. I desperately wanted to howl at it as a diversion from the craving to feast upon the people who came and went. Laughter filled the tasting room, jammed packed with wine lovers in evening dress strolling from one tasting station to the next, stopping to "cleanse their pallets" with cheese and bread in-between. Brogio had advised me that this was "part of the business."

I once again looked to the full moon that appeared to shine more brightly than days past. My mind wandered. I imagined that Brogio must be circling some delicious female, ready to entice her into the wine cellar and quench his thirst for his preferred food: Human blood. I longed to taste it with him. I held on to my blood lust, remembering

Brogio's constant coaching about control, so I wouldn't randomly attack a lone wine taster exiting the building. Every day seemed to make it easier to control my urges. Later, I planned to satisfy my hunger with the creatures in the forest. I shook my heavy coat and sat back to scratch each ear, but a shadow from the trees gave me pause.

She walked out of the forest, taking me by surprise. How had I not heard her footsteps, sensed her presence? She was the most beautiful creature I had ever seen. Dogs don't get hung up on human appearance, but even my dead veins pulsed a bit at the sight of her. She glowed like the moon. Was this . . . could it be the one the goddess told me to find?

Her slender body glided toward me. Her footsteps made no sound. She wore a steel-blue dress that matched her eyes. Her long blonde hair hung to her waist in a straight line around her. It shimmered like silver in the moonlight against her alabaster skin. I backed away as she drew near.

She stopped just in front of me. "Beautiful boy, why're you sitting here alone?"

I felt the caress of her hand. A sharp, electric thrill coursed through me. I gave her a quick "ruff."

Her laughter tinkled like wind chimes in a breeze. She mesmerized me, and I followed her into the tasting room, not considering any consequences.

*****

The room buzzed with people laughing, talking, tasting wine, and nibbling on bite-sized cheese and other assortments. In my dog days, I would have snuck a few tasty treats from the tables positioned in the center of the room, but I no longer had the desire for them. The wine stations were beautifully built mahogany bars completely against the walls surrounding the room. Each was backed with a display of the featured wine. The room's low lighting allowed each wine bar to be spotlighted and encouraged guests to move from station-to-station.

I spotted Brogio among a group of women. None of them able to keep their hands off him. One touching his arm; another rubbing his shoulder; and yet another trying to feed him cheese. I followed my mystery woman as she glided toward him, a glow appearing to surround her. I deftly avoided the slightly intoxicated guests and snuggled into a corner near the edge of a couch where I could see them both at once.

Brogio looked up and immediately spotted her. He stopped in mid-sip, dropping his wine glass and shattering it along the floor. The women next to him jumped back but he was already moving forward as wait staff rushed in to clean up the spill. The look on his face reflected how I felt after gorging on human blood: Ecstasy, wonder, disbelief, but most of all ... complete and utter love, like the love I felt for my human family. As she slowly moved toward him, he stopped abruptly, closed his eyes and brushed his fingers across them as if he were hallucinating and needed to clear his head.

When she reached him, she held out her hand. He stared at it, dumbfounded.

"Hello, are you Brogio? I was sent here to find you. I'm Selene."

He slowly took her hand, held it up, and kissed it, as if it would break. "I am ... Brogio. At your service." Violet eyes with hundreds of unasked questions pierced into steel blue ones. This had to be his Selene. The one that Kane had spoken about. I could feel his intensity. Every fiber of his being appeared to shake.

People were staring. The light that surrounded her appeared to envelop them both. A more breath-taking couple didn't exist. His neatly combed platinum hair fell forward on his brow. Her moon-colored hair shimmered at her waist. The top of her head just touched under his chin. Selene was tall, but Brogio still towered over her.

I became afraid that this grand entrance drew too much attention from the party guests. I looked up at Brogio, making steady eye contact and tried to convey a message. *Everyone is staring at the two of you. Take her aside somewhere.*

He nodded his agreement and acted immediately. "Please come have a glass of wine." He took her hand and folded it into the crook of his arm, steering her over to an empty wine station. The women Brogio had deserted stared at Selene with open hostility.

I walked across to the other side of the room and found another quiet corner a bit closer to them to observe. They only seemed capable of staring at each other. Brogio's eyes only left her to reach for a pair of crystal glasses and pour them each some sparkling white wine.

At that moment, my hackles rose. I smelled danger in every corner of the room. Time for me to patrol again. I walked the perimeter of the room, looking for new arrivals. Perhaps someone I hadn't noticed had arrived before Selene appeared. A suspicious-looking man entered but then turned to help his companion down the stairs. Searching through the crowd, I noticed a man walking toward Brogio and Selene, but he stepped to his left in front of them to greet another guest. Turning, I spotted a large, dark man standing by the wine station next to the entrance. His steady gaze followed Brogio and Selene's every move. He looked like a man who spent his time outdoors, his skin darkened by the sun. He had black hair and eyes, dark eyebrows, and a very large black moustache. His broad, tall body was hard to miss. He dressed less formally than others. He wore a canvas hunting vest with multiple pockets. His khaki pants were held up by a large belt with a silver buckle in the shape of a deer. For his size, though, I sensed litheness about him; one who might move through the forest quickly. Everything about him resembled that of a hunter, just like the ones I had seen in the woods during deer season with my human Alpha. I pushed down the growl that seeped up through my throat and backed away to bide my time. If he made a move on Brogio, I would make quick work of him with my poisonous venom.

Unless ... had this man followed Selene here? Was he her protector? Had Artemis sent them to see Brogio? I would have to wait and see.

Brogio and Selene continued to stand frozen in a corner together. I continued to watch the dark man, while my suspect stood watching my Alpha and the object of his affection. Some of the guests began to leave. Brogio excused himself from Selene in their solitary corner and stepped in the direction of the front door to thank each one. I quickly scampered to her side to protect her if needed while watching my Alpha intently.

The dark man moved to another wine station further into the room. He congregated among the last remaining 20 guests. His eyes rested on me. I detected a glint of an acknowledging smile in them. He knew I was watching him.

Brogio soon returned to Selene, offering her his arm. "Can you stay for a while?"

She smiled and looked into his eyes. "I wish I could, but I have work early tomorrow."

"Then I must see you tomorrow night, Selene. We have much to discuss in private. Will you come here for dinner at eight o'clock?"

"Yes. I would love to, Brogio. Please, see to your remaining guests. I can see my way out." Her eyes twinkled at him, and her lips turned upward in a smile.

"Wait, take my ... dog with you. He will see you out." He looked at me and gestured with his hand for me to follow here.

No, Brogio. I can't leave. You are in danger.

His command filled my head. "I know a dark one lingers, but do as I say, and make sure she gets out safely!"

I slicked my ears back and whined, but did as he said. I knew he could take care of himself if he was aware of the potential danger. At least I gave fair warning. I walked Selene to the edge of the woods, expecting her to disappear. Instead, we came upon a small blue Volkswagen Beetle. "This is my ride, doggie. Thanks for looking after me." She patted my head, leaned down and kissed the top of it, then turned and opened the car door. "Take care of your master."

I felt a sudden rush. She wasn't human; nor a vampire. Something else. It didn't matter. I loved her the moment she glided into our lives.

*****

I rushed back to Brogio in the tasting room. I found him with the dark stranger, calmly sharing a glass of white wine. I crouched in a corner to listen.

The dark man drank his wine slowly, savoring the flavor like one who enjoyed only the best. Perhaps he reveled in every moment, but a darkness seeped from the pores of his body. I could smell it. A low growl from my corner caused him to fix his black eyes on me.

"That one sees himself as your protector." He motioned in my direction.

"And you would be wise to stay clear of him, sir." Brogio's eyes never left the man's face.

The visitor threw his head back and laughed heartily. "Corso, I told you, call me Corso."

"All right, Corso." Brogio leaned closer to the visitor. "You've intruded on my tasting and enjoyed my inventory. What do you want?"

Corso smiled. "That's simple. I want to hunt with you."

"So you are a gamesman?" Brogio shrugged and took a sip of his bubbly wine.

"Yes, I have hunted all over the world. You name it; I've killed it."

"Well, unfortunately, you are out of luck. There's nothing exotic here. The forest creatures in Oregon wouldn't excite you." My Alpha stepped back as if to dismiss his uninvited visitor.

"Oh, you misunderstand, Brogio. I have something quite fascinating in mind." Corso took a step forward as if to block his host.

"Well, sir, I am uninterested in whatever it is you have to offer. I've been entertaining, and it's been a long night." Brogio turned sideways, away from Corso, and snapped his fingers loudly. Three large men who worked in the barrel rooms stepped out of the darkness." My associates will show you out now. The tasting and this discussion are finished."

Brogio walked around Corso, exhibiting the grace of a dancer. He turned as he moved away from the hunter and called out to me. "Come, Snow."

I got up from the corner where I was sitting and stepped toward Brogio. All throughout, I kept looking back to see the hunter being escorted out behind us by Brogio's men. The smile on the man's lips and the sinister glint in his eyes told me we hadn't seen the last of him.

*****

I found it impossible to rest after Corso's visit. I sensed that his presence meant us harm. Not Kindred, I guessed that his hunting had another purpose. I determined not to let Brogio go hunting with anyone but me. My need to stand guard while Brogio slept left me restless and uneasy. My loyalty was growing stronger.

The moment the sun set, Brogio leaped out of his resting place and rushed to the house, busying himself with preparations for his dinner with Selene. I followed him through the house and observed as several very large men dressed in black clothing to match Brogio's jumped to his every order. They were all of similar build and height. "I need you to get me the finest wine. Three bottles of the chardonnay, three of the cabernet and two bottles of dry champagne. The blue satin linens to match her eyes. Have the chef prepare the venison. No wait, add duck. Include all the vegetables. Dessert. One of everything." He ordered a table set to satisfy a queen. He was truly smitten by this beautiful woman.

In the old days, I would have left puddles of drool on the floor at the exquisite smell of roast venison and duck. Unfortunately, they bored me now, and I begged for a special human blood bag treat.

"Oh, all right, Snow Blood. I guess if I'm going to have a special night, you should as well." He opened the refrigerator, reached for a glass bottle and poured me a bowl of elixir. I devoured it hurriedly. These sleepless nights had left me feeling quite hungry.

I moved into the den and lolled on my bed in front of the fire, my belly gorged with the heavenly treat. The doorbell rang. I rolled over and watched Brogio leap from his big chair and rush to the entrance, perfect in his usual uniform of black pants and a turtleneck sweater. His blonde hair hung around a face full of childlike wonder as he opened the door and invited Selene inside.

She wore a silver dress and shoes and carried a matching purse. Long silver earrings framed each side of her face under her hair. The silver of her dress made her steel blue eyes even more brilliant. Brogio couldn't take his eyes from her.

"Your home is beautiful, Brogio." She explored all the downstairs rooms, and he followed behind her, proud of his elegant house with its plush mahogany furniture, textured fabric, and art that he explained to her he had collected from around the world.

"Come, sit by the fire and enjoy one of my vintage bottles before dinner. Are you hungry though? Do you want to eat now instead?"

My Alpha acted like a giddy schoolboy.

"Wine would be good. I can wait to eat when you are hungry." She sat next to his chair and took the glass of chardonnay that Brogio extended to her. She peered over the glass into Brogio's eyes. I could feel her power over him sweep through his body into mine.

"Tell me, I must know. How did you come to be here?" He moved to the edge of his seat.

"Honestly," she stared at the grooves in her glass, "I don't know."

"And yet you arrived here last night at my wine tasting, asking for me. What do you mean that you don't know?"

"Brogio, this has all been very strange. Until yesterday morning ... how can I explain this? Well, I led a normal life. I work as a nurse at the hospital. I've been here for as long as I can remember. But, I had an unusual dream night before last." She stopped abruptly and took a large sip of wine.

"Please, Selene, tell me about your dream." Brogio fidgeted in his chair.

"You're going to think I'm crazy, but in it, a beautiful woman, surrounded by light, told me to come to your wine tasting to find my true love. She said his name would be Brogio." She pushed her hair away from her face, displaying her embarrassment, took another sip of wine, and continued. "When I woke up, I felt like a different person. Oh, I mean, I looked the same, but the life that I had been living before didn't matter anymore. All that mattered was coming to meet you."

Brogio took her wine glass from her, set it down on the table, and then clasped both her hands in his. "You have lived here in Oregon all your life?"

She nodded her head and whispered, "Yes."

"And you have been in Newberg all this time?"

Again, she nodded the affirmative.

"But, we have never met? How could that be?"

Still mute, she shrugged.

Brogio's words filled my mind so that she couldn't hear. "Could this be another of Artemis' tricks? Do I even care? She has to be a doppelganger."

A dopplewhat? I sat up from my resting place.

Brogio glanced at me. "An exact double of another person. Artemis has to be behind this, but all I feel is gratitude. She's giving my Selene back to me."

Caution, Brogio. This could be a trick.

My warning was disregarded. He stood and pulled her up from her chair. "It doesn't matter how you got here, let's just enjoy our time together." He escorted her to the dining room and the lavish meal that awaited them. The acrid smell of darkness stopped me in my tracks as I followed them.

The doorbell rang just as he was seating her. I rushed the door, realizing the smell of the hunter had preceded his approach. I barked wildly.

"Snow Blood, enough. Go sit with Selene! Keep her company for a minute." Brogio called out to me as he approached the front door.

I backed away, but not before I saw Corso standing in the door frame.

"I must speak with you, Brogio." The man tried to push his way inside, but my Alpha easily held him at bay with an outstretched arm.

"Outside, Corso. I have a dinner guest." The vampire pushed the hunter to the outside with such force that he almost fell backward. My Alpha quickly shut the door, but I could hear their words through Brogio. Not satisfied to just listen, I climbed the circular staircase near the front door so I could peek out the window overlooking it. I had a vantage point from which to observe.

"I did not intend to interrupt your meal," Corso said as he stepped closer to Brogio, "but I insist you hear my proposal."

"What proposal? Come back tomorrow when I don't have a guest."

"That may be too late for your lady friend. You see, I am an impatient man, and I don't like to be kept waiting. It would be a shame if your lady had to pay for your putting me off."

His threat bristled Brogio. "What do you mean?" My Alpha grabbed Corso by the throat.

"Don't be hasty," Corso choked out quickly. "If anything happens to me tonight, she will be dead tomorrow ... Dead while you sleep. And you can do nothing."

Brogio momentarily loosened his grip on the hunter, hesitating, shocked.

"Surprised that I know you are a vampire? Don't be. Like I told you, I've hunted everything in my lifetime. Now I want the ultimate challenge of hunting you." Corso's smile widened as Brogio's fist wrapped around his throat.

The hunter choked out, "You have two days to play my game with me, or she dies when the sun is bright."

"I would rip you apart if not for ..." Brogio loosened his grip.

"Selene? Of course, I know."

Brogio pushed Corso further away from the house. "You come near Selene or me, and I will kill you."

"Well, then, there's always your dog." Corso backed away, smiling. "Two days ... you have two days."

*****

Brogio entered the front door as I rushed down the stairs. He gave me a displeased glance but returned to Selene, and I followed to sit next to him.

"Is everything all right?" Selene searched his eyes sensing his anger.

Two of Brogio's men immediately brought out a feast fit for a queen.

"Fine, it's fine, Selene. I apologize for the interruption." He poured her a fresh glass of wine and served her a generous portion of duck after seeking her preference. He couldn't take his eyes from her as she ate.

"Aren't you going to eat? There's so much food." She put down her fork to wait for him to begin.

"No, no, I'm enjoying watching you. Please, continue. I'm not . . . hungry right now. Too fascinated by your radiance." He teased her, but I knew he meant it.

She laughed out loud ... tinkling wind chimes. "Tell me about yourself."

"I live a very dull life, Selene. Wine-making is an art form. It requires ... much of my attention."

She savored her meal as he spoke. She dabbed at her mouth with the fine satin napkin. "So, how long have you been in Oregon?"

"A very long time."

"Come now, you can't be more than in your mid-to-late twenties. How could you have been here that long?"

"I'm older than I look." He gave me a sidelong glance and smiled.

"Really? You have a slight accent. Where did you come from originally?"

"Italy ... I moved here from Italy."

I couldn't resist. I mentally posed the question, *What did you do after you lost Selene?*

The silent room only held the slight sounds of Selene's fork on her plate. Brogio's words infiltrated my mind. "Not now, Snow Blood. Can't you see I'm busy?"

My playful side kicked in. *If you don't answer my questions now, I will pee on the floor ... interrupt your dinner ...*

"Fine. Ask your questions. I moved back to Firenze ... a full-fledged vampire. It's called Florence in English."

Did you create Kane there?

"I created the first vampire clan there."

How did you do it?

"Humans wanted power and immortality. The fools traded their souls for it. The curse will continue for all of us until we return to Hell to claim our souls."

Is the first clan in this Florence now?

He chuckled, but only in his head, so as not to disturb Selene. "Oh, they grew in numbers and strength. Then, infighting created civil war. Many of them left to form their own covens."

I wanted to squeeze every drop of information that I could from him while I was in control. *Do they know you came to Oregon?*

"Most of them think I'm still in Florence. Enough, Snow Blood! Let me focus on our guest."

Selene put her fork down and smiled at us. "That was the most delicious meal I've ever had! I didn't realize until I sat down that I hadn't eaten much in days!"

"Dessert?" He raised his eyebrows in expectation.

"No, I couldn't. I'm stuffed. Don't tell me you are a gourmet cook too?"

Brogio chuckled. "Unfortunately, my wine business keeps me busy. But, fortunately, it allows me the luxury of a fine chef and help with the house."

She leaned toward him. "Tell me about your life in Italy."

Brogio sat back and appeared to reflect carefully before answering her. In my youth, I traveled looking for adventure. Instead, I found love."

Selene smiled. "I thought a man such as you would have not been left to lead a solitary life."

He stared deeply into her eyes. "I lost her, and I've spent my life since grieving for her ... until I met you."

Selene took an almost inaudible breath and sat back in her chair.

He rose abruptly and helped her from her chair. They glided to the fire and sat talking for the next several hours. At various points in the conversation, they would just stop and gaze into each other's eyes longingly.

Bored, I fell asleep on my bed. When I awoke, they stood before the fire locked in a crushing embrace, kissing passionately. His mouth was on her neck, her shoulders. It covered her lips, and they both moaned as if they were in the throes of mating. Suddenly, Selene stepped back. "No, Brogio. I need to go before we take this further. I just ... I need to go."

He took a step away from her. "I'm sorry. I couldn't help myself. You are so beautiful, and I ... "

"I don't know what's come over me. I'm usually more of a lady than this. Please, don't get the wrong idea. But, it's as if I have known you ... forever." She straightened her dress and smoothed her hair.

He smirked, then raised his eyebrows skyward. "Perhaps you have."

She turned to leave, not looking back at Brogio.

I moved to block her way, worried that he had somehow driven her off. Brogio's words halted me. "No, Snow Blood. Stay!"

Brogio moved quickly and took her arm. "Please, before you go, give me your address and phone number, won't you?" He reached into his pants pocket, then handed her one of his business cards and a pen so that she could write them on the back.

"Yes, all right. I have to work a late shift tomorrow night at the hospital, but you can always reach me on my cell." She finished writing down the information and walked to the door.

Brogio followed her. "Let me walk you to your car."

I wondered what he would do to protect her from Corso's threats. Especially if he still lingered on the other side of the door.

*****

I waited near the door for Brogio's return. He walked past me, grabbed a long black coat and motioned to me. "Okay. She's in her car. We're going to follow her home. Make sure she is safe from the hunter."

We ran through the woods at super-human vampire speed, keeping her blue Volkswagen Beetle in sight at all times until we reached Newberg.

We followed the vehicle, staying out of sight, until we reached a condominium complex surrounded by a small forest. Forests surrounded almost every neighborhood in Oregon. She parked in front and went inside.

"All right. Here's the plan. We need to protect Selene, make sure that no one comes after her." He knelt next to me.

I sat back on my haunches as he continued to relay his plan.

"You guard the back; I'll take the front. I'll be here until just before sunrise. Be on the lookout for anything that might harm her. When I leave, stay here, follow her wherever she goes."

He stood, and I shifted next to him.

"Make sure she is safe. She's working late tomorrow night. Stay out of sight, but guard her. I'll take over after sunset." He knelt down again.

But why don't we track down Corso? I put my paw on his knee and cocked my head. *He threatened you and Selene.*

"I need to think it out. He did threaten to kill her. I suspect he will make an attempt on her if I don't comply to his wishes soon. He gave me two days." He stood up. "Now go around back."

*****

The night remained quiet. And the next day and evening were mainly uneventful. No sign of Corso at the apartment building. Brogio joined me at the hospital just after sunset when Selene had gone in for work. We stayed out of sight, hiding in the parking lot behind a car next to her Volkswagen. She emerged before sunrise. She came out the rear exit dressed in green hospital scrubs. She got into her car and drove off. We followed on foot and watched as she stopped at a small all-night convenience store and bought a half-gallon of milk and some laundry detergent. After that, she headed back home.

Brogio had told me that his intent was to see her safely inside, then head home to rest before the sun rose. He was cutting it close, though he insisted on staying on stakeout for as long as the darkness prevailed. I would stay and guard her again once the sun came up. My hunger ate at me with no time or opportunity to hunt. It was excruciating.

85

Just as Selene gathered her bags from the car in the parking lot, we spotted it: A giant black werewolf on a dead run at her. It climbed over cars and smashed in windshields as it charged in her direction. In a heartbeat, we both transformed. Brogio morphed into the same ravage beast he had been the night of my death. I could feel my body growing as I lunged forward at the intruder with him.

Selene was shutting her car door when the beast sprang at her. She screamed and dropped her bag on the pavement, laundry detergent spilling everywhere. Brogio leaped and intercepted the werewolf just inches from where Selene stood.

The two creatures tumbled through the parking lot, teeth flashing, red eyes glowing. The Brogio demon instantly sprang to his feet as the werewolf threw its large body at him. Gracefully, Brogio evaded the werewolf's attempts to engage him by merely stepping back at superhuman speed. Again, the sense of a mongoose goading a cobra. The demon Brogio cocked his head at the werewolf and spread his arms wide, taunting his opponent. The werewolf sprang as Brogio closed his arms around it. They again tumbled to the concrete. I leaped into the fray and took a large bite from the attacker's shoulder. The taste of flesh and blood quenched my hunger pangs. The bite wound debilitated the werewolf enough for Brogio to finish the job. I tumbled off the combatants, turned quickly in their direction, and crouched for my next attack. It was not needed. Brogio snatched the werewolf as it crouched on the pavement, picked it up over his head, and literally broke the creature's body in half before our eyes. Its blood drenched us all.

Selene's screams sliced through the early morning air. Lights from the surrounding dwellings popped on. She backed away from us terrified. And then it happened. Her terror ignited our need to comfort her, and we both transformed, still covered in blood. Brogio's clothes had fallen away in shreds at his transformation, and he stood naked before her.

She stopped in mid-scream, confusion and disbelief spreading across her face. Brogio took a step toward her, a hand outstretched, and she shrunk from it, horrified that he might reach her.

Brogio's voice sliced through my brain. "Get rid of the body!" We both turned to the spot where Brogio had thrown down the broken werewolf. The body was gone!

The sun's faint rosy glow began to spread across the sky with its first warmth crawling over the pavement toward us. My Alpha hesitated a second, then turned and commanded, "Guard Selene!" before taking off and vanishing on a dead run.

Okay, I answered. *But you must think of what to tell her. How to explain all this*. I swiveled back to her to see the incredible shock in Selene's eyes.

*****

Selene scampered into her unit, her shoulders slumped, still crying. She slammed the door leaving me outside to

87

examine the area where the werewolf had been. Only blood remained where its body had fallen.

Could Corso have removed it? Was the creature Corso? Could it have survived? I didn't dare leave Selene to investigate.

I looked around to make sure no one was observing me. I knew only one way to get rid of the blood on the pavement. I did what any blood-thirsty vampire dog would do and licked it up. Not my choice. It tasted of death but I gagged it down anyway to protect against any consequences.

I returned to Selene's door, and her soft sobbing surrounded me. Lights went back out in the surrounding residences once the commotion had calmed. Two men came out from their residences. Discovering the damage to the cars, they rushed back into their condos. I assumed to call the police.

I rested on Selene's front stoop. Just a big dog napping on her large "Welcome" mat. I imagined the wolfman crawling away into the woods, its broken body twisted in agony. Would Corso have waited to see the outcome of the werewolf attack?

I dozed in and out, but my senses trolled through every sound, any movement and best of all, each smell. No danger lurked this day. Only the unrelenting crying of a woman who had suffered a life-changing shock.

When the distant police sirens alerted me, I crept behind the building. People gathered in the parking lot in disbelief at the damage to the cars. One man shrugged and got into his unaffected car and drove away. I shrunk further from sight as more activity came with the progression of the day. Enraged neighbors filed complaints about the damage to their cars. After being questioned, others either left or went inside their homes. No one seemed to notice the faded spot where I had licked up the werewolf's blood.

Lingering on her back porch, I heard Selene stirring in mid-afternoon. The sound of water, and then the rattle of things in what must have been the kitchen brought me closer to her back door. I pushed my body into the wall next to her glass sliding doors, when suddenly she opened them and stepped out onto the patio.

She jumped when she realized I was pressed against the wall. Her blue eyes seemed to grow two-times larger.

I whined and put my paw up to her, trying to appear adorable and non-threatening.

She took a step away from me in disbelief. I stretched out and slowly belly-crawled toward her.

"What are you?" She backed away until the back of her knees hit a patio chair, and she fell into it.

I stopped and stared directly into her eyes. Cocking my head, I whined again and backed away, trying to show I meant her no harm.

We sat in this manner for a very long time.

Finally, she spoke. "You've been here since last night?"

I crawled two steps forward and whined.

A long silence followed. Selene was holding her face in her hands. Finally, she looked up at me again. "You don't mean me harm, do you? You want to help me?"

Another step and whine.

"Are you guarding me from something?"

I crawled to her feet, stopped, and licked her bare toes.

"But, you were ... he was ... those things?"

I sat up and continued my steady gaze into her eyes. The hunger I began to feel had to be contained. She is not human. Grateful that I didn't sense her blood, or her humanity. I knew I had to feed in the forest soon.

She must have known that she would get no answers from me. She leaned forward and patted my head. "Thank you for saving me from that other thing ... this morning. Whatever that was."

I placed my large paw on her knees and looked at the patio doors. She followed my gaze.

"You want me ... inside?"

I got up, walked to the door, and then returned to her.

"For my safety?"

I repeated my walk between her and the door. She got it. When she went inside, I sat next to the sliding door, and she dropped to the floor next to me and again stared at me, lost in thought.

Brogio arrived as the sun set. In his haste to arrive here, I noticed his black clothing looked rumpled and less meticulous than normal. I immediately blasted him with the questions that had been formulating all day, since our mental connection was less frequent while he slept. *Did you see anything on your way to your rest? Did you see the werewolf or Corso? Could the werewolf be Corso?*

He placed his large hand on my head. "I barely had time to make it back to my resting place; darn nearly burst into flames! No time to hunt for Corso, or the wolf. My primary intent is for us to guard Selene." He motioned to her door. "Thank you, Snow Blood. Go, hunt and rest. I will guard her throughout the night."

Selene saw him through the patio door and appeared to steady herself for what must come. She opened the door for him and took a step back. He didn't move.

"I need you to invite me inside, Selene."

She picked at the threads of her cut-off jean shorts and looked at the floor. "Why should I let you in?"

"I think you know why. May I come in?" He didn't make a move.

She hesitated, and I took the opportunity to try and understand. *Brogio, you can't go into homes where you are not invited?*

"Yes." He responded. "And neither can you, or any of the Kindred."

Selene's voice shook as she responded to his question. "Yes. Come in." She moved further back into the room, lifting her head defiantly as he entered.

"First, I can assure you that the thought of hurting you is not within my reasoning." He stood just inside the door.

"What are you? What are you both?" The words escaped from her lips in an almost desperate plea to avoid the truth.

"You know what we are. You saw us this morning."

"No, you can't be those ... things ... you broke that other creature in half! How can beings so beautiful ... how can you be those ... beasts?" She buried her face in her hands and began to cry again.

"Don't you know, Selene? You knew me in another life. Don't you think that's why you are here now?

"Another life? My strange dreams. Nightmares. The woman in the light ... what is happening here?" Her eyes pleaded with his to know the truth.

I so wanted to hear their conversation to fill in the gaps that I had yet to learn, but my hunger pulled at me forcefully.

Brogio moved through her back door. "Come. Sit with me now. No harm will come to you, and I will tell you our story." He turned back to look at me, then at the woods behind me, and commanded me to go hunt.

I turned as if I would leave but circled back and pressed against the wall near the door. My need to hear their story outweighed my hunger.

Selene didn't speak but remained silent as he began.

"I was Ambrogio then. Italian. Carefree and as I told you, an adventurer. It was more than a millennium that I traveled to Greece to have my fortune told by the Oracle of Delphi."

I could hear him pacing as he spoke. "Delphi was home to the great temple of Apollo, the sun god. And home to Pythia, the Oracle, who would speak prophecies inspired by the god. I was told I would be cursed. Alarmed, I couldn't sleep that night. I sat outside the temple all night thinking about what might be in store for me. When the sun rose, I walked back toward town. That's when I saw you dressed in white robes. You were a virgin maiden in the temple and took care of the Oracle while in her entranced state. The Oracle was your sister."

"Wait!" Selene's voice interjected. Are you implying that I am that person?"

"Yes, you are her down to the last detail."

"Brogio, how is that possible? Selene's agitation was apparent.

"Hear me out, Selene. When I saw you, my life changed. I approached you in that moment and introduced myself. I met you every day at dawn before you entered the temple. Soon you loved me as much as I loved you. I asked you to

93

marry me and return with me to Italy. You agreed, and we were to meet at dawn the next morning near the temple."

Selene remained silent. Too shocked to respond, I imagined.

Brogio sighed and continued. "Apollo had been watching. He'd had his eye on you and was enraged that I would take you away. He appeared to me at sunset that night and cursed me."

"How did … he … curse you? Did he … did he make you this creature?" Selene's words came in short spurts.

"From that day forward his sunlight would burn my skin." He began to pace again. "I was beside myself. I wasn't able to meet you at sunrise as promised. I somehow found Hades, god of the underworld. He listened to my story and made me a deal. Steal Artemis' silver bow for him, and he would grant us protection in the underworld. He gave me a magical wooden bow and arrows to hunt with. I was to offer his hunting trophies to Artemis to gain her favor and steal her silver bow. I had to leave my soul as collateral until I brought him Artemis' bow. That way, if I didn't succeed, I would have to live in hell forever, without you. I had no choice and agreed."

He stopped, and Selene questioned him. "What happened then?"

"I had no way to contact you. I had parchments but no writing implement, so I took his bow and arrow and killed a swan. I used its feathers as a pen, and its blood as the ink and explained I couldn't meet you but would find a way. I left the note in the meeting place before sunrise and fled from it. You had no choice but to keep working at the temple so not to anger Apollo further. Each day you returned to our meeting place and found a love poem from me. This went on for 44 days. I would slay a swan and use its blood to write to you. Then, I offered the body of a swan as a tribute to Artemis, the goddess of hunting and the moon and Apollo's sister. I hoped if I couldn't steal her bow she might convince Apollo to remove the curse. On the 45th day I only had one arrow left, missed a shot at a swan and had no blood to write to you or anything to sacrifice to Artemis. I became distraught. Artemis, seeing how dedicated a follower I had been to her came down to me. I begged her to let me borrow her bow and arrow to kill one last bird and leave a final note to you. She took pity and gave it to me. Out of desperation, I ran to Hades, but Artemis realized what was happening and put her own curse on me. The curse caused all silver to burn my skin. I immediately dropped the bow and fell to the ground in agony."

Selene murmured to Brogio. "What you went through is unbelievable."

Brogio continued on. "Artemis was furious with me, but I begged for forgiveness, telling her about the deal Hades forced me to make, Apollo's curse, and my love for you. She took pity on me and gave me a last chance. She offered to make me a great hunter, almost as great as she, with the speed and strength of a god and fangs with which to drain the blood of beasts to write my poems to you. In exchange for this immortality, I had to agree that you and I would escape Apollo's temple and worship only Artemis forever. I left you another note telling you to meet me on a ship at the docks. You found it and met me there before Apollo noticed. When you arrived at the dock, you found a coffin with a note telling you to order the ship's captain to set sail and to only open the coffin after sunset. You did, and when you opened the coffin, you found me alive and well."

"Where did we … where did you and your Selene go?"

At that moment, Brogio stepped through the glass sliding door and glared at me. "Go, feed! I need you here when I leave!"

I jumped at the chance to satisfy my blood lust and leaped into the joy of chasing my prey. Though I wondered how the story ended and what Selene's reaction would be. Whether she would be accepting of Brogio, or repulsed.

＊＊＊＊＊

It took a large deer in the forest around Selene's home and then a mountain lion in the surrounding woods of Brogio's estate to sate my thirst. I circled a wild pig to top off my meal, when I sensed that I was no longer the hunter but the hunted. Five pairs of red eyes glared at me from various points in the woods. A female werewolf and her pack surrounded me. I instantly leaped through a small area that they had left open and took off running toward the house. I felt them at my heels, teeth chattering, ready to slash my throat.

I could only hope these werewolves didn't know these woods as I did. I leaped over a large crevice filled with tall silver blades that were buried at the bottom. This trap had been the death of a number of out-of-town deer hunters, Brogio had told me. A surprised yelp reached my ears as I sped ever faster forward. Brogio had recently booby-trapped the opening just for an occasion such as this. One down; four to go. I could feel the alpha female gaining on me. Quite a clever girl to let another take the fall for her.

A quick right turn, then another took me inside a hunter's blind where huntsman hid and awaited their prey. I watched as they all sped by me. It wouldn't fool them for long, but it would give me enough of a head start in the opposite direction. It also bought me a moment to catch my breath.

I turned away from our house and ventured deeper into the woods than I could remember. My search for higher ground led me to a steep incline just north of a clearing in the trees. I waited for the werewolves to spread out so I could take them one-on-one. My anger brought on a full transformation, and I jumped one of the males as he searched directly beneath my vantage point. The element of surprise enabled me to rip out his throat, disengage his head, and then, his heart. I slung it aside, then scampered deeper into the woods. Three left.

I kept running, knowing that a moving target is harder to attack than a sitting one. Brogio's voice invaded my mind as I sprinted down a dirt path.

"Take out the alpha, Snow Blood. The others will retreat if you do." Thank the gods he could read my mind and know

I fought for my life. He was trying to protect me, even from afar.

I came across a pile of fallen evergreen branches lying on the ground. Again, I hid until I spotted the three of them running in my direction. They separated, and the Alpha female was alone. She sensed me and turned just as I launched myself into her. My demon-self outweighed her. We rolled over and over, teeth chattering, claws extended. One roll too many, and she was on top of me. I threw her out and away from me, avoiding a sharp, poisonous bite. I leaped to my feet and circled around her. Crouching, I sprung, biting her on the shoulder and ripping part of the muscle away. Her blood flowed profusely, and she gave out a low scream. I spun around to re-attack. She tried to turn and defend herself. Before she did, I pounced on her back, took her down, and rolled her over on her back. I desired to tear her throat open; finish her off. But before I could, my venom brought her into the same convulsions that had occurred before with the intruders in Brogio's wine cellar. Her last spasms left her lifeless. Slowly the wolf transformed into a human. A tall, slender female brunette. So, my toxin works on werewolves as well as humans, I wondered in my mind.

The remaining two werewolves crashed through the woods, skidding to a stop at the sight of their leader's dead body. They both threw back their heads and howled. Whining and backing up, they fled feeling the disconnect, I guessed, from their dead leader.

I worked the rest of the night to dig a hole deep enough to bury the now human bodies of the three dead werewolves. Like the alpha female, the other two had gone back to their original human forms upon their death. They had been young male adults. I left the one in the crevice where he had fallen deep into the earth. Remorse spread through me. I knew their deaths couldn't have been avoided, but my defensive actions sadden me just the same.

Suddenly, I felt Brogio's pull on me. "I'm glad that you are safe. Come to Selene's now, Snow Blood. I must go to my rest. Time for you to guard her."

I looked up at the sky. Sunrise was hastily nearing. I took off running yet again in the direction of Selene's apartment building. While in stride, I pondered the events: the attacks on Brogio, Selene, and now me. Why? Why had Selene, his Selene, been sent back to him? Was this simply a distraction for Brogio in an attempt to weaken him?

*****

Another day passed with me guarding Selene. As sun set, I left her after she entered the hospital for her overnight shift. It seemed like the safest place for her to be left unguarded, given all the people inside the hospital, plus the security guards at the door. I rushed to the wine cellar where Brogio would soon rise from his daytime rest.

He awoke with a vengeance. His purple eyes were filled with blood. He commanded me to follow. We both could smell Corso's presence and hear him pacing as he awaited us at the end of the driveway to the estate. We spotted him exactly where we had anticipated. Corso appeared to shrink significantly as Brogio stopped directly in front of him. My Alpha towered over him, almost leaning into him.

99

The hunter stepped back to allow himself some space. His air of confidence returned. "What is your answer, Brogio? Will you hunt with me to save those you love? Time is running out for all of you."

Corso clearly failed to realize the mood of his intended target. His taunt pushed the already vengeful vampire into action. Brogio grabbed the hunter by the throat with his left hand, ready to rip it out. He placed his right hand atop the man's chest, ready to tear out his heart as well.

Corso struggled to breathe. He was dangling in the air, being held up by Brogio's left hand. He was starting to gag, when he managed to weakly cough out a few words. "Careful, my friend. Remember, there are others who will tear out her heart if harm should come to me."

The message sunk in, and Brogio abruptly dropped the huntsman to the ground. "Who sent you here?"

"Who? I told you, my good man. I merely wish to hunt with you." Corso struggled to his feet.

"You mean, hunt me!" Brogio's malevolent stare should have been enough to send the man running, but he held his ground.

"Yes, and you shouldn't test the resolve of those more powerful than you." Corso drew himself up to try and match the vampire's height as he spoke the words.

"Someone more powerful? Do you mean the gods?" Brogio couldn't hide his suspicion that Artemis or perhaps even Apollo might be the driving force behind these attacks.

"I know nothing of gods!" Corso spit out. "But know that I have been blessed with certain powers and friendships that will make our hunt more interesting."

Magic? He means he has magic, Brogio. That's how the werewolf disappeared! I placed myself next to my Alpha out of concern for him. He needed my protection more than ever.

Brogio glared at the man, and in a low, controlled voice replied, "What are the terms of your hunt."

"Ah, wonderful. Tomorrow night. I'll even give you the advantage of hunting you in your own forest. But no transformations into demons. Your extraordinary vampire skills against my magical hunting skills." The hunter smiled down at me with malice in his eyes. "I will, of course, use any weapons of my choice to kill you."

It's as if he heard my thoughts!

"Done!" Brogio replied with force. But, before the hunter could depart, Brogio reached out and grabbed him by the neck yet again. Gradually, he tightened his grip until Corso's face turned beet red. Corso's strength was no match for Brogio. His punches to Brogio's shoulders did little to earn his release. Then, one more surprise. Brogio took a bite and a long drink from Corso's neck.

Corso screamed in pain. Struggling, his legs kicked wildly into Brogio's chest and legs. My Alpha didn't seem to notice.

Brogio spit out Corso's flesh. "You said nothing about revenge for being bitten and dined upon, you stupid fool!" Brogio leaned in and licked the freshly opened wound, then dropped the man in his tracks. "Hopefully you will have regained your strength by tomorrow night." Brogio laughed as he headed back to his home.

I was tempted to finish off the hunter, but feared the possibility of serious consequences as had been promised. I didn't want to be responsible for an attack on Selene. Instead, I followed Brogio home.

*****

Once inside the front door at the estate, Brogio turned to me, his face still contorted in anger from the confrontation. "First off, I have summoned Kane to come."

Why? I can help you. Why do you need him? He'll only make you angry again.

A quick knock on the door interrupted my thoughts. Suddenly, Kane entered the front door, flashing his usual mocking smile. "At your service, my master! I left as soon as I felt your summons." Ever the dandy, he wore a three-piece gray suit with a red tie and matching handkerchief in his breast pocket. He did not look dressed for a fight.

Brogio swiveled toward me. "I've already apprised him of the dangerous situation, Snow Blood." He then patted Kane on the shoulder with a fatherly greeting. "Kane, I need you to go tomorrow and bring Selene here. I've spoken to her, and she will be expecting you. Guard her with your life. I don't trust this huntsman, or whoever brought him here. She must be safe at all costs. Do you understand?"

Kane couldn't help himself from torturing his father. "Perhaps I might have a small dalliance with her while we wait? I mean, if she's as hot as you say ..."

"Touch her, and it will be the last thing you ever do!" Brogio spun to tower over his offspring.

"All right, all right! Understood. Guard the hot chick."

"Snow Blood, you will go with me tomorrow night. But you must keep out of sight. I see no problem with overtaking this *hunter*. But if for any reason, should higher powers be involved, just bite him. Your venom will do the rest."

"Wait, what?" Kane was intrigued. "What about his venom?"

"Not now, Kane. I must think. The two of you must pledge to me that you will care for Selene above all else!"

I walked between them. *It's doubtful that Kane will think of anyone but himself. But you can trust me to protect her with my life.*

My Alpha placed his hand on my head and rubbed it in a rare display of affection.

"Well, I can't imagine that you won't be victorious, Brogio, but of course I will take good care of your lady." Kane laughed softly to himself and strolled over to the den table to pour himself a glass of the ever-present wine.

"No time for drinks, Kane. We all need to gorge on blood tonight to enhance our strength for tomorrow." Brogio was ripping his clothes off as he headed for the front door.

"To the hunt then!" Kane stripped out of his stylish clothes, dropped them on the den chair, went out our front door, and morphed into a red-eyed gargoyle with wings! He screeched at me as he lifted himself into the air. I was discovering that I didn't need to always become a demon to hunt and dine on my prey. I followed close behind, howling at the moon as we scoured the woods.

* * * * *

I was surprised and impressed when I accompanied Kane to collect Selene and bring her to the estate. He wore a navy blue three-piece suit and matching tie, looking more conservative than I had seen him in our previous interactions. Just after the sun set, he knocked on her door with me at his side. He didn't ask to be invited inside.

Selene's eyes registered alarm until she saw me standing next to the man at the door. Kane explained gently that Brogio had sent him to protect her during his battle with the forces that threatened us all. "Come with me to the estate. Brogio begs you to accompany us."

I wagged my long tail profusely to signal that it was all right.

"Yes, Brogio told me on the phone. But, how ... how long will I be there?" A typical female question.

"Pack an overnight bag. Think of it as a mini-trip." Kane smiled. "We will wait for you here. But, please, hurry. We have very little time."

She headed inside to what was likely her bedroom and packed a small suitcase in record time. Kane carefully gathered the bag and smiled at her. "Forgive me, but we need to make haste. It will be faster if I carry you so that we can move at vampire speed."

Selene stared at Kane. "What does that mean?"

"Why, it means faster than lightning!" Kane laughed.

She nodded, and he scooped her up in his arms.

"Don't be afraid; hold tight!" Moments later, he was racing through the woods with me fast behind him.

I splintered off once we reached our grounds, only pausing to locate Brogio with my senses. The sound of footsteps startled me. I hid behind bushes and turned up my listening skills. Twigs snapped under someone's footsteps. And then the sight of Corso in a tan hunting outfit. He carried a double crossbow loaded with silver tipped arrows. A large coil of silver chains hung around his shoulders.

He stood perfectly still at the sight of Brogio in a small clearing about twenty feet away from him. "Ah, so you had no trouble finding me then."

Brogio did not respond, and the hunter approached him cautiously. "Go ahead, vampire. I will give you a head start." The statement was almost a boast.

Brogio, scoffed. "I need no head start, you idiot!"

Corso immediately fired two arrows at Brogio, who dodged them by using his superhuman speed. He sprinted into the woods laughing over his shoulder at Corso. "So I guess the hunt has begun?"

But then something unexpected happened. Corso vanished into thin air! Magic!

I put my nose to the ground to scent out my Alpha. He was near the same gully that I used when the werewolf pack was chasing me. *Can you really use this cunning trap for the hunter too!*

Brogio materialized, standing close to the edge of the trap and easily dodging the flying arrows aimed his way. He waited.

The hunter stopped, sensing something not quite right. Corso moved to the edge of the gully, stumbled slightly, regained his balance, and backed away deftly. "That might have worked in the past, vampire, but not with me."

Brogio ran 100 yards with his lightning speed, coming to a rest in a tree top with an easy view of the woods. The hunter again vanished.

Brogio's voice slid through my mind. "The angry gods have given him magic, Snow Blood. It must be Apollo, or Artemis, or both who want us all dead. This could be trouble."

What can I do? Let me track him and use my venom to kill him!

"Do not worry, my friend. I will handle this."

I ignored his command, sniffed the air, then put my nose to the ground, picking up both Brogio and Corso's scents. They may be able to instantly vanish, but my sense of smell gave me a powerful advantage.

Corso reappeared just 20 paces in front of me searching the trees, then suddenly disappeared again. After only a few minutes, he reappeared. He tracked the ground to pick up clues. This was repeated several more times.

He can't hold his invisibility, Brogio! Only for a few minutes at a time. That clue was enough to give my Alpha the edge he needed.

Brogio waited for the hunter to circle just underneath him. He had remained perched high up in a maple tree. At last, Corso's invisibility wore off. Brogio leaped from the top of a tree, slamming Corso's shoulders with his feet and stunning the hunter, knocking him to the ground. Brogio fell upon him, used his sharp nails and fangs, and attempted to rip open his rival.

The silver chains wrapped around the hunter appeared to come alive. They slithered like snakes and curled around my Alpha's throat, burning into his neck! He screamed out in obvious pain.

They were twenty feet from me. *Brogio! I'm going to save you. I can't watch this for much longer.* My mind reached out to him.

"Wait! Stay! Not yet!" His mind pierced mine.

I cringed to see the silver, like an acid sunlight sinking into his skin, scalding his throat. The hunter leaped to his feet, firing arrows into Brogio, who was unable to avoid them this time as he struggled to tear the silver chains from around his neck.

107

Badly burned and wounded, with a half-dozen arrows in him, Brogio summoned the tremendous strength that had grown for thousands of years within him. He struggled to his feet, gave out a mighty scream, then tore off the chains and flung them aside. They appeared to wither into the ground. In another movement, almost faster than my eyes could detect, he grabbed Corso with his burned left hand and ripped out part of his throat with his fangs. At the same time, his damaged right hand tore out the hunter's beating heart while his brain was still alive to watch in horror. Brogio took a bite of it, blood spurting everywhere.

Relief flowed over me as I watched the hunter's destruction.

With his last breath, the hunter screamed in terror. The look in his eyes reflected his own death. He had been defeated at his own game.

Brogio ripped out the burning arrows from his own body. I rushed to the dead man, hoping to drink the hunter's blood only to be repulsed by the smell of death. I suffered from the unfortunate distaste to drink blood from a dead body.

Brogio lifted Corso's body and carried it through the woods to the gulley the hunter had avoided earlier. I followed, curious to see how he would dispose of it. He threw the hunter's body into the pit where it was impaled on the sharp, upturned spikes. Taking a pack of matches from his pocket, he lit one, then set the pack on fire and tossed it into the pit on top of Corso. The flame simmered for a brief time, then caught onto the hunter's clothing. We stood and watched as the fire consumed his body.

"Let's head home, Snow Blood. I will send my men to fill in the hole with dirt and disguise its existence."

Upon arriving at the estate, Brogio made a detour to his bedroom, and I followed. He quickly ripped off his torn, bloody clothes in his spacious bathroom and stood before a full-length mirror to inspect his jagged and burned throat and damaged hands. "It's already healing, Snow Blood." He touched the damaged areas gingerly. The arrow punctures were almost completely healed. "Consuming Corso's heart will make for a quicker recovery."

I watched as he took a long shower, a mixture of his blood and Corso's running down the drain. Brogio playfully motioned for me to join him for a rinse. I sat back on my haunches and refused to be enticed. *Your spirits are high now.* I watched as the wounds on his neck completely disappeared in the shower. I wondered if this was how it looked when he healed me after I'd been hit by his car.

"Yes, why not? Another foe is vanquished, and we are all safe, at least for another day." He shut off the water, stepped out of the shower, toweled off, and went to his closet to carefully inspect his wardrobe. I wondered why he even bothered with careful selection. They all looked the same to me.

But ... He blocked my thoughts.

"Yes, I know. She is not safe. I don't know what's worse. Her having to fend off Kane's constant advances or ..." His thoughts trailed off, and he ran his hands through his long blond hair to shake the water from it. A sad expression spread across his face.

When he joined our companions downstairs, Selene ran to Brogio, relief written over her face. Kane shrugged and went to open a bottle of wine, pouring them all a glass. "Before we toast to your victory, tell us what happened." Kane handed each of them a hefty portion of red wine in a trio of crystal goblets.

Brogio accepted his glass. "I think that's something Selene doesn't need to hear, Kane. Let's just say that while Corso was bestowed with some magical tricks, I prevailed. It is apparent to me that he was aided by a powerful entity."

Then, he turned toward the kitchen. "Wait one moment. We can't forget Snow Blood." He quickly returned with a human blood bag and poured it into a bowl for me. "To success!"

Brogio smiled quizzically at Selene. "So tell me, were you able to hold Kane off sufficiently?"

She laughed. "He is persistent. But, I prevailed!"

Kane scowled and muttered, "She must be befuddled to choose you over me."

Brogio's laughter echoed through the room. "Sit. We have something to discuss."

I made a bee-line for my soft bed. Exhaustion began to creep through my body. The others sat as requested.

"I think the gods are attempting to put an end to me and those I love."

"Which gods?" Kane interjected. "Apollo? Artemis? Hades?"

"Perhaps. None of the gods have ever favored me. I have no proof. Just suspicion. In the meantime ..." Brogio swung his gaze to Selene and took a deep breath. "I have to send you away, Selene, to keep you safe. Kane, I'll ...

"What? No! I won't go; can't go!"

I jumped up from my bed, surprised by the emotional shock wave that pulsed through the room. *I was supposed to find the woman surrounded in light. Why would Artemis send her to you? Why would you send her away where we can't protect her? Brogio, you're not making any sense.*

He remained silent, but I could see the determination in his face.

EPISODE FOUR
Rebellion

"**B**rogio, why would you want us to be separated?" Selene stood up and began to pace back and forth in the den of Brogio's house. Her agitation consumed the room like a thick smoke. It was getting me a bit choked up. "Are we not safer together?"

I observed the conflicting emotions spreading across Brogio's face as I stood on my bed by the fire.

Kane intervened. "Look, Selene, it won't be so bad ... I mean you, me and Snow Blood, of course." He gave me a smirk as if to let me know my presence wouldn't matter to him.

"That's just the point, Brogio! Can't you protect me better than Kane? Selene wrung her hands in frustration. Her pacing continued, her heels clattering against the limestone floor.

Brogio stood and tried to quiet her fidgeting hands by taking them in his. "Selene, as long as you are with me, you will be an easy target for someone to use against me. Kane and Snow Blood are worthy opponents for any would-be attacker. But, I mean to draw our enemies' focus away from you and on to me."

She appeared at a momentary loss. Then, I detected a flicker of mischief in her eyes and awaited her next tactic. "Truth be told, Kane's unwanted suggestions are wearing thin on me. I'm not sure that we can trust him alone with me for much longer."

There it was. She played the jealousy card.

Brogio gave Kane a sidelong glance and then smiled back at the object of his affections. "Don't worry. Kane would never do anything to seriously incur my wrath!"

I sat back down on my bed awaiting her next move.

"I ... I know that I am crazy to feel the way I do with all the chaos and violence that surrounds you, but I don't feel safe with anyone but you. It's as if I didn't truly exist until I met you."

I watched Brogio's face as he tried to control his impatience. This was a man who did not handle being disobeyed well. He had always been in control of his destiny since becoming Kindred.

"Selene." Brogio spoke in a calm tone. "It's for your own safety. How can I protect you if you won't work with me? You will have both Kane and Snow Blood to guard you. They are fine protectors."

I got up and moved to Selene's side, all the while sympathizing with her. *Why did Artemis tell me to find the one who glows like the moon only to have you send her away!*

His thoughts thundered back at me. "Quiet, Snow Blood! You must help me in this matter!"

I sat down hard, back straight, chin raised to meet his eyes in defiance.

"Oh, for the gods' sakes, Selene!" Kane moved toward us with an outstretched hand. "I am perfectly capable of taking care of you." He glanced at me. "And the dog, too."

Doubtful. I wished I could have made him hear me.

Before I knew what literally hit me, Brogio merely swiped his arm from me to the wall. The intense force threw me against it. I was on my back looking at the ceiling. I scrambled to my feet. Brogio loomed over me. The act of being thrown didn't hurt, not physically.

"You will NOT disobey me, dog!" Brogio turned from me to Selene. "Please trust me in this, Selene. Your safety is my upper most concern, and I need you and Snow Blood to comply!" He stomped off upstairs and slammed his bedroom door, frustrated that Selene and I dared to question him.

I sat next to the wall, amazed I felt no pain, and watched as Selene quickly turned to Kane.

"Don't you see? I can't leave him. I ... I am bound to him. I don't know why, but I just am." She began to pace once again. "How can I have feelings for such a creature ... for any of you ... is beyond my understanding, but I do."

Kane sighed and walked over to the mahogany bar in the corner next to the fireplace to pour a glass of wine. He sat on a tall stool and rested his head in his hands. At the same time, Selene came to me, bent down to hug me, and whispered, "I can only guess that you were standing with me, Snow, and for that Brogio punished you. Thank you for supporting me." She squeezed me tighter. "We're safer if we're all together."

I whined and licked her face. When she stood, I began to lick my paws, trying to overcome the indignity of being hoisted across the room.

I suspected that Selene was the embodiment of Brogio's long-lost love, but he appeared almost weakened in her presence. Why was this? I had to know more.

$$*\ *\ *\ *\ *$$

Brogio finally emerged from his bedroom. It was just before the rising of the sun. As he hurried down the stairs, he gave me strict orders to stand guard over Selene while he and Kane slept the daylight away in their casks.

Selene kept inside the house, afraid to venture out. Not that I would have let her out of my sight.

She busied herself by filling up a deep bath tub with water, then forced me to endure a wash down. Like my old Alpha once said: "I would have rather stuck needles in my eyes." I hated the smell of perfumed soap, bubbles, and hot water, but I did rather enjoy her scrubbing my chest and ears.

115

After toweling me off, she headed downstairs to the kitchen and set about cooking her dinner. I did a perimeter check around the estate just as the sun was setting, then went to find Kane. I had to know why Brogio acted in such a curious fashion around Selene.

I waited for him at the entrance of the wine cellar.

Kane and Brogio emerged from their resting place, and Brogio walked over to me and placed his hand on my head. I sensed it was his way of apologizing for his anger. He then headed toward the house and Selene.

Kane, on the other hand, emerged ready to hunt. He removed his clothing at the entrance, but didn't immediately transform as he dashed into the woods. I soon caught up to him and watched him track and take down a deer and a boar. Inspired, I broadsided a doe and her baby and drank my fill of blood.

It was at some point here that I thought about Tommy, the little boy I used to live with. His favorite movie was a cartoon called Bambi about a deer and his family. I had a momentary feeling of remorse, but rationalized that the baby was better off dead than living out in the wild without its mother.

I returned to the estate and intercepted Kane just pulling on his clothes outside the entrance to the wine cellar. I had to make him understand what I wanted. I tried to force my mind into his. First, I sat in front of him, willing him to hear my thoughts.

Why is Brogio so childlike with Selene? They were married. What did you mean they were chaste?

He stared at me with blank eyes. "What in hell's name do you want, dog?" He tried to move forward, but I placed my formidable body in front of his.

Again, I sat down patiently in front of him. I looked at the house and then back at him.

"What?" Kane stared at me with a puzzled look on his face.

I looked up at the moon, then back at the house, and made a whining noise. *What happened between Selene and Brogio?* I concentrated as hard as I could.

His eyes widened, as if he had heard me for an instant.

"You want to know ..." He scratched his head.

I moved eagerly toward him and barked.

"You want to know ... what?" Kane's eyes met mine.

I forced my mind to reach out to his while staring deeply into his flickering eyes. There had to be a way to make him hear me.

"You can't compel me, dog. Only my maker can."

I focused harder, my eyes never leaving his.

"Brogio? About Brogio?"

I anxiously barked, looked at the moon and back at the house.

117

"And Selene?"

I leaped excitedly in front of him and barked three times.

"Ah, you want to know why he's a blithering idiot around her, right?"

This time, I sprang up and down like a yo-yo, barking my head off.

"I have no idea why I am having a conversation with a dog. But telling that story would give the old man a blistered hide. Let's go back to the house. I'll pour me a glass of wine, and you and I shall have a little chat."

I had done it! Kane had heard my thoughts! Or, at least he had deciphered my dog code.

* * * * *

The house was quiet, except for some intermittent stirring of pots and spoons from the kitchen where I had last left Selene, when we entered. I could hear Brogio murmuring softly to her. The vampire appeared to focus only on Selene when she was around. I wondered if this meant that Brogio could not hear my thoughts while consumed with Selene.

I settled on my bed in front of the fireplace in the den eagerly wanting to discover more about Brogio's strange behavior. Kane sensed my anticipation for what he had to tell me and took a torturous amount of time to fill his wine glass.

"All right. It's fairly simple you see."

118

It might have been simple to him, but he needed to spill it so that I could form my own opinion.

"Artemis let them be together as man and wife ... but like I tried to tell you before Brogio stopped me, she placed a condition on it." He took a long sip of his wine, and I was growing impatient.

"A virgin goddess expects her followers to be chaste."

Again, that word. What the hell did it mean? I tilted my head in both directions to show him I didn't understand.

"Ah, okay. You don't know what that means. Well, quite simply put, my boy, it means he couldn't mate with her. Think about it. You see a bitch that you want to take. You know, put your seed into her. But, you aren't allowed. Not only are you not allowed, there's no touching or feeling or any affection. Get the picture?"

It hit me like a bolt of lightning. Brogio was in complete lust. Like a dog in heat without a mating partner. I jumped up and chased my tail in excitement for a few seconds. Kane's boisterous laugh halted the conversation in the kitchen.

"That's right. He's been waiting thousands of years to have this woman. Now, she's here in the flesh, and all he can think about is climbing on her and marking his territory!" Kane snorted and laughed out loud, but it sounded like he was a dog in heat himself!

I thought to myself, we are dealing with a demon who is so in lust that he doesn't have his senses about him. This can't bode well for his decision making.

Kane's voice cut through my thoughts. "Ah, but I need to finish the story for you." As the years passed, Brogio's immortality kept him young, but Selene continued to age as a mortal. She finally fell ill and was dying. Brogio knew that he would not join her in the afterlife because his soul still resided in Hades. At night, he killed a swan and offered it to Artemis, begging her to make his wife immortal so they could be together forever. Because the goddess appreciated his years of dedication and worship, she made him a last deal. He could touch Selene just once, to drink her blood. Artemis told him doing so would kill her mortal body, but from then on, her blood mixed with his could create eternal life for any who drank it. She said she would see they stayed together forever." Kane stopped and took a long draw from his wine glass.

I sat mesmerized by the story.

Kane took a deep breath and continued. "Of course. Brogio wanted to refuse, but after telling Selene, she begged him to do it. She is his one true weakness. He bit her neck and took her blood into his body. When he set her dead body down, Selene began to glow with light and rose to the sky. Brogio could only watch as Selene's spirit lifted to meet Artemis in the moon. When Selene became a part of the moon, it became even more brilliant than before. So, Selene became the goddess of moonlight. Every night she would reach down with her rays of light to the earth and touch her beloved, as well as all their vampire children who carry the blood of both Brogio and Selene together." Kane stood up, finished his wine, and stretched. And then he said something I wouldn't have expected from him. "This

Selene, if she's his Selene, is his one chance at true happiness. We need to help him however he needs it." He turned and strolled into the kitchen.

I sat in stunned silence, feeling immense sorrow for them both. No wonder my Alpha was behaving oddly around Selene.

*****

Selene sat at the table in the dining room of the estate surrounded by three demons of sorts. She had made enough for everyone, not knowing how to handle mealtime with us.

"Selene, you need not cook for us. We can only be sustained by blood, and that includes Snow Blood." Brogio pulled over two wine glasses. "Will you be comfortable with us partaking in blood as you eat your meal?"

She shifted slightly in her chair at the realization of our consuming blood in front of her. I watched the emotions flutter across her face and then a steely resolve set in. "Yes, I know. Do what you must. I guess I have much adjusting to do with all of you." She amazed us all a few moments later when, after looking down at me, she excused herself from the table and then returned with a bowl of blood that she set on the floor for me. She smiled at Borgio and then confessed. "I realize that life may never be the same for me. It's time for me to toughen up."

Selene ate a hearty meal of her own making. A chicken breast, sweet potatoes, a large salad and garlic bread. The smell of the garlic bread made my stomach turn. Back in my dog days, it had the opposite effect.

Brogio stared at her like a lovesick moose. His violet eyes gazed into her steel blues. He found it difficult not to watch her every movement. It sickened me; who knows how it made Selene feel? But given what Kane had just told me, I wanted them to have a happy ending.

Selene wiped her mouth delicately with a lace napkin and leaned in Brogio's direction. "Please don't send me away. I want to be here with you. I wouldn't be willing to adapt to your lifestyle if I didn't."

Brogio was shaken out of his compliant mood. He straightened his back as to fortify himself against her. "No, you will only be safe if you can't be harmed as a result of my being hunted. Right now, things are still . . . dangerous. We can't take any chances."

"But isn't there some sort of strength in our numbers, together?" She tried to reach for his hand, but he stood up from the table.

"Selene, if something happened to you because of me, I wouldn't be able to go on with this existence." He ran both his hands through his pale hair and sat down again. "I've been without you for eons. Now that you are here, I don't think I can go back to the life I had before. Don't you see that this is the only way? You, Kane, and Snow Blood need to go into hiding. I am the target. No need to put you in the line of fire too."

I got up from the floor and walked to Selene's side. I couldn't help but to take her side of this argument. I set my gaze on Brogio. *We all take our strength from you. Can't you see how weakened we will be without you?*

"Enough, dog. I am master here." He shot back telepathically as he gritted his teeth, his fangs dropping slightly.

Kane leaned back in his chair, smiled, and stretched his legs out in front of him while he sipped his wine.

"Brogio, I am not going to leave you!" The woman was adamant.

Nor am I, my Alpha.

Brogio looked at Kane, who only shrugged back at him. He pounded his fist on the table. "Do as I say, all of you! It's for your own protection."

Selene stood and walked around the table, and I followed her. "Why won't you listen to reason? Are you trying to sacrifice yourself to save all of us?"

Brogio sighed. "If it needs to be done ..."

"No." Her word was cold and clear. "We won't let you do that. If we go down fighting, I want us to be together."

My master ran his hands through his long pale hair again, then looked at each one of us individually. He appeared to be in disbelief at the defiance he was hearing. Kane kept silent, which seemed to be another vote in our favor.

"All right! Disobey me! Then, I will leave all of you and take the danger with me!" He turned and moved to the door in a blink of an eye.

We all stared at the open door as he stepped through it. There was no stopping Brogio. No time to react.

*****

Selene stood with her arms stretched out after him as if to somehow bind him to her. Kane simply shook his head. I sprinted after him. I just couldn't sit still at a time like this, even if I had been commanded to safeguard Selene. I ran the boundary of the property but could pick up no scent of him. I sprinted down to the lake and found no trace of Brogio. I frightened the night creatures in the woods as I dashed recklessly between the trees, crunching leaves and breaking twigs. I cared not if I disturbed my usual prey this night. I ran to the open field where I had first seen Artemis. Nothing. His scent had simply dissipated on the front door step.

I returned to find a dejected Selene being consoled by Kane in the dining room. He stood behind her with his hands on her shoulders. It might have been entirely innocent, but I could take no chances. I walked up to him and delivered a warning growl.

"What? I'm only trying to comfort her. She's really tense." He stared at my eyes directly.

My growling increased, and he backed away. Selene remained clearly distraught. She bolted from her chair and ran up the stairs, slamming the door to the bedroom that

Brogio had given her on the night that he had defeated Corso.

Again, Kane shrugged. "It's useless, dog. She's hopelessly connected to our dear father. While you were gone, she asked me to help her find him. When I explained no one has been able to find him when he decides to disappear, she even *turned on the charm to convince me to help her.* Not wise, I think. I'd like to take advantage of her, but I'd end up suffering the true death."

We sat for a long time in silence until the sun rose. Kane abruptly stood. "Rest time, dog. I've got to recharge my batteries. Keep watch of Selene."

I padded my way up the stairs to lie in front of my charge's door. Soon, I heard her stir. I scratched at the door to let her know I was on the other side. The deadbolt clicked, and Selene knelt down and wrapped her arms around me.

We stayed there for a long time in silence. Then, she stood and motioned for me to follow her. She sat down on the end of the high canopy bed and patted it, signaling for me to join her.

I settled in next to her. She whispered, "Snow, we have to find him. I am bound to him. I need to be with him. I feel this love for him that I can't explain … Her words trailed off. She stared off into space, drawing within herself. Then, reaching some inner resolve, she took my face and looked into my eyes. "Kane is going to block my efforts to find Brogio. We'll leave tomorrow and travel during the day when Kane can't follow us. Brogio keeps telling me that I am

125

his original Selene. If that's true, we will go to places to jog my memory. Perhaps if we get closer to where he has gone you can sense him, or track him. We'll go to Italy. That's logical." She sighed. "What's illogical is that I've known Brogio for five minutes but feel like it's been a lifetime. I know we'll find him. What do you say, Snow?"

I licked her face and answered with a low, "Ruff!"

She spent the rest of the day arranging more time off from work and travel and airfare to Italy for both of us. She didn't venture downstairs when night fell. After packing her small bag, she declared we would be up early to catch an early morning taxi to the airport. She soon slept deeply one arm thrown over my back. Her resolve to search for Brogio gave her peace.

I admired her determination but sensed this plan would endanger her. The results might lead us into the danger Brogio was trying to avoid.

I could try and find him, but this time I sensed if he didn't want to be found I would have no luck. But, what if I could reach him through telepathy? Perhaps, he would not think of blocking me? Perhaps I might read his mind?

My musings were interrupted by a light, almost like a moon beam, shining straight into my eyes. Then, the silky voice spoke. "Come to me, Snow ... I will help you."

I pulled away from Selene, jumped off the bed, and ran through the open bedroom door and down the stairs. I stopped only to leap up on the heavy front door and pull down on its latch, leaving the door wide open. I knew I shouldn't leave Selene, but if Artemis could help us ...

Kane, who had risen from his sleep, called to me from the wine cellar entrance. "Wait, dog! Where are you going?" I could hear Kane's footfalls behind me.

I followed the voice to the open field near the house conflicted by my need for help, and my fear for Selene. I now understood that Brogio had been dealt a fate that forced him to live as a monster. But he had protected me and shown me kindness. Inwardly, he still held on to his human characteristics and felt love for those under his protection. Somewhere between my mistrust of him and his unselfish need to protect Selene, Kane, and me, Brogio had truly become my Alpha. I had to do whatever it took to protect all of us.

*****

She stood tall, surrounded by her light in the open field. She appeared more beautiful each time I saw her. Her pale skin and long flowing hair always changed in color according to the phase of the moon. Her eyes were the purest of blues, and I could not look away from her. The animals of the forest—deer, squirrels, boar, even the rats in the field—stood outside her circle of light, paying homage to her. I ignored my blood lust for all the delicious prey sitting there for my taking.

I scooted to a stop outside her light circle. Kane, who had been trailing me, skidded abruptly next to me.

"What the hell is going on, Snow?"

"Come, Snow. Come inside the light to me." She beckoned, and with a dainty paw, I stepped into her circle.

Kane tried to follow but each time he lifted his leg, he was sent back, unable to cross the threshold of light.

"Not you, abomination! You may listen but not enter!"

As I walked across from darkness into her sphere, I felt my entire body lighten. My thirst for blood left me, and I was almost a normal dog again. I halted in front of Artemis.

"See what it will be like to be my companion? No more hunger, no more trials. Just peace. Comfort. And, of course an undying devotion to me."

Her offer was tempting until she mentioned the undying devotion part. I shook off her words and tried to get to the point. *You said you would help me. Can you tell me where Brogio has gone?*

"Of course I can." Her radiance brightened. The silver dress she wore shimmered. Gold and blue highlights cascaded down in waves of rolling color.

Then, please, tell me. He may be in danger.

"What will you give me in return?" Her inner light brightened.

But, you said you wanted to help. You sent Selene to him. Don't you want them to be together?

"What I want will make no difference to you, Snow. You will belong to me in the end."

The thought of belonging to her frightened me. If she wanted to help Brogio and Selene, why had they been subjected to such misery? And, what would she do to me? *Please, my goddess. Help me. They need to be together. It has been too long for them.*

"Would you sacrifice yourself to help them?" The bright light within the circle almost blinded me with her question.

What do you mean?

"I want you to come freely to me whenever I command it. To give yourself to me as you have to Brogio." Her words sent shivers through me.

What will that mean?

"It means you will be my companion for eternity. You will do so willingly, happily, and I may make you into any form I desire."

Do you mean I will be your mate? I am just a dog. Why would you want that? My shock must have been obvious.

"If I so desire. All I know is that I want your loyalty to belong to me, not him. Do you agree willingly?"

Should I say yes? I could say that I would, then deal with the consequences later. Or, I could avoid her command with Brogio's help. Assuming I could find where he had gone. I had to take the chance. *Yes, my goddess. I agree.*

The explosion of light at that moment totally blinded me.

"Very well then. He has gone to Florence. He is in the place where Kane was made. He will know." With those words, Artemis began to swirl. The lights surrounding her spiraled upward, turning first red, then orange, then gold. Silver shimmered through gold as the goddess began to fade. The light surrounded me like a caress, and then darkness overtook the fading light.

I felt a moment of shock at her leaving. The realization that I had lied to her hit me. How could I hide something like that from her? She appeared to know my every thought. Perhaps it mattered little to her what I planned, but more what I had agreed to do? What if I couldn't prevent fulfilling my promise to her? What if she could read my thoughts?

I turned to Kane. For the first time since we had met, he stood speechless. His pale skin appeared even whiter. He composed himself as I approached.

Finally, he spoke up. "That was unbelievable! She let me hear the telepathic conversation between the two of you!" He turned around and threw up his arms in amazement. "That bloody goddess wants you for herself! Unbelievable. Wait until Brogio hears about this!"

I raised my head and growled a warning at him.

"Do you mean to tell me you don't want him to know?" He stared deeply into my eyes.

I growled and bared my fangs at him.

"All right, all right. Calm down. You have your reasons." He stood up tall. "Besides, it's nice to have something on you in case I need it!"

I had no doubt that he would use it at the first opportunity. Kane seemed like the opportunistic kind.

But why had she let Kane hear the conversation? Brogio and Kane had both warned that the gods were sneaky and selfish. What else did she plan?

I sat in front of him and tried again to make my thoughts known to him. *Where in Florence were you made?*

He looked deeply into eyes. "You're trying to tell me something again, aren't you?"

I barked.

"It has to be about Brogio's whereabouts? Right? I heard her tell you that I would know ... my birthplace, so to speak."

I leaped in the air barking.

"Ah, that's it. It's the St. Regis Hotel in Florence. That's where I ... that's where my transformation to vampire took place."

*****

We returned to the house, after a quick stop for dinner in the woods. I went to the balcony off the large kitchen. I needed to be alone and concentrate on trying to reach Brogio. I sensed he would be angry by my threatening him, but I had to try. His sudden abandonment felt just plain wrong.

I stood quietly for a long time, gathering my strength. And then I blasted out my thoughts to his faraway location. *Brogio, please. Listen to me. Brogio ...*

I waited but heard no response.

Again, I focused. I knew that he could hear me, no matter how far away. *Brogio, please answer me ...*

Silence.

Brogio, if you won't respond to me, I will bring Selene to you in Florence. To the St. Regis. If you leave, I will track you and find you!

His words screamed in my head. "How do you know my location?"

It doesn't matter. But the gods know where you are. They know where Selene is. If you don't want her to be in more danger by traveling to you, then come back to her!

The force of his wrath in my head almost knocked me down. "How dare you defy me, dog! I am your master! You will endanger Selene if you try to bring her to me!"

I staggered against the waves of anger he shot into my head. *And yet, that's what she wants. She is determined to find you and is ready to leave in the morning. This is her idea!*

"Why is she doing this, Snow Blood? Why are you helping her?" I could feel his resolve fading.

Because Selene needs you. Some part of her must know the love you had for each other all those years ago. We all need to be together to fight this thing. Don't you see that it doesn't matter where we all are? If the gods know, so will the evil that we fight. The gods aren't on your side. They always have hidden motives. Don't they?

"How did you get to be so logical, Snow Blood?" I could feel his sadness.

Perhaps it has something to do with my being of your blood?

I could feel the remainder of his resolve dissolve.

"I will let Kane know that I am returning and to tell her to wait for me. Stay on guard until I return." His voice was a whisper and then gone.

*****

Kane pounded on her bedroom door and woke Selene before sunrise. "Wake up! I have something to tell you!"

I stood beside him and let out a large "ruff." Disheveled, she opened the door and gave us a puzzled look.

Kane pushed his way inside and pointed to her small bag. "No need for this. Brogio is returning."

Selene turned and stared at me with a question in her eyes and then turned back to Kane. "How do I know you aren't lying to prevent me from searching for him?"

Kane let out an exasperated snort. "Because he just *told me to tell you he is coming back!*"

133

Selene turned back to me in the doorway. "Is this true?"

"Ruff!" I trotted to her and stood up on my hind legs and licked her face.

"So see? No need for unnecessary travel today, my dear." He turned on his heels and headed down the stairs and out the front door.

Selene sat down on the bed and stared into my eyes. "I have no idea what you did, but I think you are responsible for bringing Brogio home." She hugged me close and whispered, "Thank you."

*****

Brogio returned two nights later. Selene couldn't contain her excitement. She threw herself into his arms before he could pass through the hallway into the den where we spent most of our time. Brogio smothered her face with kisses, then locked her in his embrace planting a passionate kiss on her mouth.

Kane and I left the room to give them some privacy. Kane took off on a dead run, and I followed. I wondered if Brogio's intimacy with Selene was disturbing to him. Selene and Brogio's passion for each other was such that if a female of my species had been anywhere near, I would have been sorely tempted!

We scavenged through the woods, looking for creatures to satisfy our blood lust. After taking down several large deer, we felt sated enough to stop and rest.

Kane leaned back against a large ash tree. I sat facing him.

"What now, Snow Blood? Will we stay here and wait to see if there will be more attacks on Brogio? Should we split up and go elsewhere?"

Not that I could answer him, but at that moment Brogio's voice penetrated my skull. From the looks of Kane, he experienced the same thing. "Where the hell are the two of you? Come home now!"

We dashed back to find Selene sitting on my Alpha's lap in what I liked to think of as "our den" next to the fireplace. Brogio had removed his long coat and jacket. I noticed he wore a white open collared shirt and black leather pants and boots instead of his usual turtleneck sweater. Selene had rolled up her jeans to show off long slender but finely muscled legs. Her blue sweater hung off one shoulder and accented her eyes.

We settled across from them.

"I've discussed it with Selene, and I think we need to leave this place for now. If we keep moving, at least we won't be such easy prey." He kissed Selene's bare shoulder and then stared at us for reaction.

"I'm game." Kane sounded enthusiastic. "Never could stay in any one place too long."

We are all safer together, Brogio. I licked a small spot of blood from my left paw and gazed into his eyes.

135

"Very well." His eyes covered Selene's long legs in her tight jeans. "No need to take clothing, Selene. We'll buy what we need."

What will happen here while we are gone? I wondered if it would somehow be overrun by our enemies.

"Not to worry, Snow Blood. The winery will run as usual. I have ... people who serve me well and will protect the estate and the business. Let's go now."

Startled, Selene sat up. "Now, you mean right now? When we talked about leaving, I thought it would be in a few days. I need to put in a transfer at the hospital. I mean ... I took some personal leave time when I first came to this estate, but I need to let them know. And what about my condo?"

"Selene, your safety, the safety of all of us is more important than anything else right now. Trust the bond that holds us all together. It's true that we were man and wife in another lifetime. I can't leave you here at the mercy of the gods. Vampires though Kane, Snow Blood, and I are, we would never harm you. Only die trying to protect you. If we stay together, you will need to trust me to take care of you. Allow me to take care of your needs. You will no longer need to work. We will no longer live separately."

The gentle manner in which he spoke to her impressed me.

She remained hesitant. "But, I need to let them know ... at work, I mean." She was overwhelmed with our imminent and sudden departure. "I've worked too hard in my education and my career to just throw it all away; to disappear on them without a trace."

"Selene, it is my guess that you truly didn't exist here in Oregon until the night of your dream about coming to meet me. As I've explained, Artemis took you from me those thousands of years ago and placed your energy in her moonlight. It is possible that Artemis implanted the memories you have."

I whined, confused by this explanation.

"I know you've told me ... but my life up until now seemed so real. It's the here and now that seems like a dream to me." She stood, somewhat agitated, next to his chair.

"It's simple." Brogio stood and took her face in his hands. "Will you allow me to protect you? Will you trust that none of us in this room will ever do anything to harm you?"

I wondered if he was compelling her.

Brogio answered by letting me hear his thoughts. "I would never compel her. I want her to be with me of her own free will."

She stared at him. "I don't know why with all the violence that surrounds you, Brogio, but I do trust you."

"I will have someone take care of your work and your condo tomorrow. Your residence will be shut down, packed up, and stored. This is not the time to worry over a job when your life is at stake. When this is over, you can retrieve whatever your heart desires." He gave her a smile that brightened her mood.

His gaze then focused on Kane and then to me. "Are we all together in this?"

Brogio had saved me or protected me on more than one occasion. I knew I was better with him than alone. I stood and signaled my acceptance by walking over and sitting next to him.

Kane stood. "We are bound, my father. I will be with you as long as you need me."

Brogio put his arm around Selene's shoulders and held his arm out toward the room where the large black car awaited us. They moved toward it, and Kane and I followed. I looked back once wondering if we would ever return.

*****

I wondered why we took the car to our new location. Then, it occurred to me that it had to be for Selene's comfort. We drove all night, stopping before sunrise at an elegant farmhouse that Brogio must have prepared ahead of time. It had coffin-shaped containers in a root cellar that provided safe resting places for Brogio and Kane, and a room filled with antiques and a large canopy bed that Selene offered to share with me. I was to be her protector during the day. Brogio wouldn't discuss where we were going. I just knew it was north, and that the people with heavy accents he spoke with didn't sound American.

The next night, it was a short trek into a place called Kelowna. Selene leaned forward in her seat on the passenger side of the car. "Kelowna. This is British Columbia, right?"

Brogio nodded.

Kane jumped in. "Another of Father's wine estates, I presume?"

His inquiry was met in silence, so he babbled on. "I know you have holdings here. I was bored one evening while you were gone, so I snooped through the files in your desk. It's on Okanagan Lake. Name comes from Okanagan. Means grizzly bear. Hmmm ... I wouldn't mind a bit of bear."

Kane's comments were met with silence. Selene turned back to us and smiled. "Tell us more, Kane. It sounds interesting."

"Well, some claim that a lake monster named Ogopogo lives in the lake." He chuckled. "Some trying to disprove it have said it's just a beaver, or a log. But the local tourism makes use of the legend. There is supposed to be a children's park with the creature's statue in it." He sighed. "Lots of tourism here. Maybe we can make use of it."

"Enough, talk, Kane. Along with the Canadian Rockies, there's a sport and music festival here that draws more than 25,000 people, but we won't be partaking in any of them. We have to lay low."

"I hear that like Forks, it's not as sunny here as in other parts of the country in the winter, or the summer! Give me gloomy overcast skies any day!" He popped a flask of blood and drained it. I licked my chops in anticipation. "I think your dog is hungry, Brogio."

I whined, and Brogio pulled over in a wooded area. Kane pushed open the door, and I ran through the forest, capturing several small rabbits to quench my snack-attack. Back in the car, I licked my chops, dislodged some fur from my teeth, and then settled down for a nap. I wondered how Brogio could go so much longer without blood than Kane and I could. My thoughts strayed to a time when I was a peaceful house pet. What would Tommy think of the murderous beast that I had become?

I soon felt the car turn abruptly. I sat up to see where we were going. Kane murmured "Mission Hill Winery. Yours, I presume?"

Brogio remained silent.

The car felt bumpy along a long cobblestone path. I could see that the estate was another of my Alpha's unique architectural designs. Several men in the ever-present black turtleneck and pants stood outside the large house, as if they knew we were coming. They sprang to open all the doors and helped Selene with her small bag. I wondered if Brogio already had clothing here and how his solid black would suit Kane.

Brogio quickly circled the car to take Selene's hand. "Come, my love. Get acquainted with your new temporary home."

Selene looked up at my Alpha with a questioning look. "Temporary?"

"Yes, love, we can't afford to stay in any one place for too long. This is going to be our life for now."

She held back for a moment. Uncertainty spread across her face. Then, she nodded in a quick agreement and stepped forward.

To my utter surprise, the house was identical to the one we had left. It featured another winery. Brogio seemed heavily invested in the wine business.

His thoughts pushed into my mind. "Yes, I have wine estates and businesses all over the world. If we keep moving, you will get to see them all."

He looked up at the sky and then to his men. "Take care of my lady and Snow Blood. It is time for Kane and me to retire." He then turned to Selene, took her face in his large hands, and stared into her eyes. His mouth crushed down on hers, and she responded by wrapping her arms around his neck and kissing him back, pushing her body into the curve of his. Kane turned away from their public display of affection.

"I will see you tonight, Selene. He turned to me and pointed a finger in my direction. "Snow Blood, stay with her until I awaken." He patted me on the head as he walked by, then slapped Kane on the back and pulled his first son close to him. "This way, Kane." Selene and I followed a tall, pale man into the house.

We settled into one of the sumptuous bedrooms as the sunrise spread through the windows. One of the men in black brought Selene a tray of assorted breakfast treats. The servant took a bowl off the tray and placed it on the floor. Then he poured me a flask of fresh human blood. I lapped it up quickly, then settled at the end of the bed, sated and euphoric, while Selene enjoyed the food on her tray. Soon, sleep washed over me.

The field was full of light. The goddess pulled me closer to her, wrapping her arms around me. Her affection made me uncomfortable. I wanted to rip open her throat but couldn't guess at the consequences. Soon, she whispered. "Beware. He is coming for all of you, my Snow Blood. I can no longer reason with him. His hatred for Brogio consumes him. He would have the beautiful one for himself, and, perhaps even you. I can't let that happen. Stay vigilant."

I sprang awake and jumped off the bed. The sunlight poured through the large windows. Selene slept like the dead. She was trying to adjust her sleep patterns to Brogio's. As for me, I slept whenever I could.

Had it been a dream? Or had Artemis come to me in a dream? It was a warning. Who was coming for us? I had to find out.

*****

The next evening, Brogio took us on a tour of the estate and the winery. It was familiar to us all as it was identical to the one in Oregon. The house and winery were surrounded by a vineyard. At the lower end of the property was a very large and deep lake, separated from the estate by thick woods. We all remained alert. Kane and I both volunteered to regularly patrol the estate.

Brogio wouldn't allow Selene to be left alone. I was the logical choice to stay with her, while my Alpha and Kane set a series of traps in the woods to lure and snare whatever creatures would try an assault on us. When they were completed, Brogio showed Selene and me where each was located so we wouldn't fall victim to them.

"We dug pits with wooden stakes buried upward to impale our prey. We covered them with screens and hid them with moss and brush."

Kane proudly interjected. "It was my idea to snare our enemies by their ankles and pull them upside down. Each trap has one." He walked to one nearby tree. "Small pieces of fern-like material are hung on trees to the right of the traps to warn us of their location."

During the day, as my little pack slept, I tried to summon Artemis in my dreams. Each time, I would concentrate so hard that I would fall asleep, only awakened by nightmares filled with faceless demons.

On the fifth day, I sat by the window in the bedroom I shared with Selene. I focused on what I had learned about Artemis from Kane. She was goddess of the hunt, wild animals, wilderness, childbirth and virginity. She protected young girls and was a perfect markswoman with her bow and silver arrows.

As I concentrated, a large deer appeared to me at the edge of the woods. Unlike other deer that stayed away from the grounds, this one crept closer. It didn't escape me that deer were sacred to Artemis. Was this her way of summoning me?

I scampered out the bedroom, down the stairs, hastily opening the front door with one large paw on the latch. I ran to where the deer had been, but it was nowhere to be found. What if it were a trap? I shouldn't have left Selene. I searched further for a few minutes but found no trace of the deer. Worried that Selene was unprotected, I scampered home and up to her bedroom.

I found her resting on the bed where I had left her. I was relieved that she was unharmed during my momentary indiscretion. But I couldn't let go of my need to protect the house from potential enemies. I went back to the bedroom window and peered outside. The oversized deer appeared to me again. It has to be a trap! I told myself. I ignored it, went back down the stairs to the front door and shut it, then returned to the bedroom. I curled up on the bed next to my charge. I would warn Brogio when he woke from his rest. I tried to stay awake and alert to the impending danger but something pulled me into a deep sleep.

*****

The darkness was filled with the silhouette of a deer. Its form blinded me. Was this a dream? A waking dream? The form dissolved and soon the goddess stood in a field surrounded in a light so intense that I could not look into it.

The two words she spoke sent me into darkness again.

"My brother."

*****

The hand on my shoulder gently caressed me. Selene's soft voice hummed a sweet tune. My eyes fluttered, and I could see the sun setting through the window.

"Snow ... Snow, wake up. You must be exhausted. Poor baby. You're always alert when I waken."

I tried to shake away the pain in my head. What were the words? "My brother"?

I descended the stairs with Selene, who was met by Brogio. It startled me to see him just as the sun slipped below the horizon.

He greeted her warmly, then looked into my eyes and sent his silent question to me. "You have learned something, have you not?"

He was eager to confirm his suspicions.

Yes. The goddess came to me in a dream. She said two words.

Before I could say them, Brogio uttered, "My brother." He snarled aloud. "So it is Artemis' brother, Apollo! He has been behind all the attacks on us! He must have known that Artemis was going to send Selene back to me. Some strange game between the two of them, no less. Everything has to have been an attempt to keep Selene from being with me. But why has she favored you with this information, Snow Blood?" He announced his question to the room.

Kane strode in with his first cup of blood. "Simple, Father! She must be sick of the mortal men and women she has always fancied."

I shot a warning glance at Kane.

He shrugged. "Err ... Snow Blood could be considered wildlife. Perhaps she sees him as one of her beloved subjects?"

"But, if I had a brother, I would want to support him. Wouldn't this goddess be on her brother's side, supporting him?" Selene interjected.

"Not necessarily, my love. You see, even though they are twins, the both of them are impulsive and vengeful. And selfish. If Apollo has gotten in the way of something she wants, she would work against him." He ran the fingers of both hands through the long pale hair on either side of his face, tucking it behind his ears. "And I wouldn't want her as a mortal enemy. She's most likely the greatest hunter of all time."

Selene touched his arm lightly. "But what does she want? Does she want you?"

Brogio threw back his head and laughed. "Oh, I seriously doubt that. I'm not her type, but I think she wants to control the two of us!"

This topic could lead to my last meeting with Artemis, so I changed it.

If it is Apollo, how could we fight him? He is more powerful than Kindred, isn't he?

He stared at me and answered aloud. "I'm not sure, Snow Blood. I think we just have to see what his next move will be. We ..."

"Brogio!" Selene interrupted. "It's impossible to follow conversations you seem to be having with Snow! How are you communicating with him?"

"You are right, my love. We are linked telepathically. Kane and I are as well. Snow Blood's question is how do we fight Apollo." He cupped her chin with one hand and kissed the end of her nose. "We have prepared the woods."

He turned to Kane and me and commanded, "Everyone keep watch."

*****

We didn't have to wait long. We were all walking toward the den when blackness shrouded the waning light receding through windows of the house. Two large crows threw their bodies against the windows on either side of the front door with a force that didn't match their size. Suddenly, every window in the house was pelted by crows. Several windows shattered. The horrific sound startled Selene, who let out a loud scream. The hackles stood up on the back of my neck.

Kane ran to a large unbroken window near the front door. "By gods! The trees, the fields are filled with thousands of crows!" He shouted over the sound of what seemed like a million birds pounding against the large house.

"Makes sense," Brogio shouted back. "The crow is his bird." He ran, pulling Selene behind him. "Come, quickly! There's an underground passage in the floor to the wine cellar. It should be safer down there."

Kane followed shouting. "Where are your men?"

147

"In the wine cellar!" Brogio spat back quickly.

Brogio pulled Selene behind him. Glass tinkled. Crows rasped their maw of a battle cry. Kane yelled "Watch out!" as three huge birds attacked Selene, landing on her back and head. I lunged for them, snatching them from her bleeding head and back. Brogio turned invisible and used his super speed to attack the throng. Headless, rabid birds started piling up and blocking the wooden floor door leading to the underground passage. The invisible Brogio must have extended his formidable demon claws to decapitate the onslaught. Headless bird bodies flew left and right. Selene ducked under me. I hadn't noticed that I'd transformed again, but my mass grew to a size where her whole body fit. Kane, in a movement that left a sound barrier trail, grabbed the handle to the door to make way for our escape underground. More birds poured into the room only to fall dead in piles on the floor. Then, Brogio screamed. The high-pitched sound pushed at my body. I dug my claws into the wood. Selene's ears and back were covered with blood. I had to fight my urges from trying to drink it. It made no difference that she wasn't human. Kane lifted the human-sized door to our escape route and held it up. Flying birds bashed into the side of the wood slate. Brogio stepped behind me and let out another supernatural scream, creating a vortex that swept the crows aside, pushing their flight back. Those close to him exploded on impact.

I froze in amazement at his ability to make a sound so shrill that the bird's body parts would break into pieces, but not harm the rest of us.

"Brogio, come on!" Kane held the door open. Gathering my wits, I pushed Selene along and followed her down a dark hole, sniffing along to detect everything around us. I looked behind us to see Kane shove Brogio down into the cellar in front of him and slam the trap door above us. Thuds against the floorboard stopped as it shut.

*****

The next thing I knew, we were inside the wine cellar. Brogio had already returned to his human form. Kane, on the other hand, had not transformed during the attack. With the excitement dissipating, I could feel myself slowly transforming back into my dog size.

Brogio's men ran to greet us. The one who had brought breakfast to Selene and me spoke first. "We tried to get to you, master, but the crows pelted the wine cellar door!"

"Brogio ignored him. "Get some water and a clean cloth so that I can clean the lady's wounds."

Once he had completed the task, he bit his wrist. "Drink this. It will heal you."

She took a step away from him. "No, not yet. I will be fine."

I could see the uncertainty in her eyes again.

"It will do nothing more than heal the scratches. I would never do anything against your will."

She shook her head. "Please. I'm fine."

He shrugged and turned to his four men. "Stay here. I may have need of you later." He walked forward and motioned for us to follow. "We can't stay trapped in the cellar forever. There's an escape hatch on the other side of the wine cellar that leads out into the woods. Follow me."

Once in the woods, we carefully made our way around the traps we had set. Near the edge of the lake, Brogio halted and instructed us to do the same. "Moving from place to place will not protect us! Apollo will find us no matter where we go ..."

His words were drowned out by the roar of a beast unequaled by any other. It began rising from the lake just a football field away from us. The monster furiously shook the water droplets from its body.

Brogio moved us all behind tall shrubs to assess it. "I have no choice. I fight him here."

"No!" Selene begged.

"This makes sense, Brogio!" Kane grabbed his maker's shoulder. "This must be the lake monster! Could it have been Apollo all these years trying to catch you here?"

"Kane, stop with the nonsense. I need to figure out how to defeat a god who won't perish." Brogio shrugged Kane's hand away.

The creature emerged from the lake. It was similar to the panwere that first attacked Brogio the day he hit me on the road. But this one could only be described as monstrous in size and shape. The creature's almond-shaped eyes surveyed its surroundings. Ugly beyond belief, with a downturned mouth and cleft head, it looked like a combination of a cat with deformed human characteristics. Large growths covered its enormous chest and back. I wondered if they functioned like body armor.

"You can't fight this thing, Brogio!" Kane's voice was filled with concern. "It's a were-jaguar, a lycanthrope. Its bite is lethal. I encountered them once in Romania. One of my coven died in agony from its bite."

"Like Snow Blood's?" Brogio sounded proud.

"And it can move between worlds. That's what we learned in Romania." Kane's words interrupted my fascination with the creature that had to be head and shoulders taller than my Alpha. More like a tanker truck than anything. "How the hell do we fight that?" Kane snorted, almost at a loss at what to do.

Kane continued to urge his father not to fight. His hands were on his hips in defiance. "Plus, the damn thing is supernatural as well. Leave it to Apollo to shape shift into this thing!"

"We don't know if it's Apollo, or a creature under his direction." Brogio focused fiercely on his most current opponent standing next to the lake a hundred yards away.

Selene turned to Kane and placed a hand on his broad shoulder. "How do you know all of this? Since when did you become an expert on this stuff?"

"Since Brogio started getting stalked. I made it a hobby to read up on anything that might attack us. I've found some fascinating reading on the Internet!" He shrugged and smiled, pleased that she had noticed his knowledge on the subject.

A noise in the distance alerted the monster, and it turned and ran along the lake away from us with a speed that matched my master's. A fallen tree lay in the middle of its path. The creature stooped, lifted the massive trunk with its deformed human hands, and threw the broken tree with a deafening scream through the woods, almost as a warning to anything lurking about.

"My gods!" Kane whispered under his breath. "I bet the bastard can bench press a car with one hand!"

"Silver will bring it down, Kane." Brogio muttered. "Wounds from silver heal at human speed. It's the only metal that can pierce its body."

"Well, try and get close enough to it." Kane snorted, a trace of sarcasm in his tone. "That thing can hear a person's pulse just by standing nearby. It'll detect Selene for sure. It can track in the dark by scent."

"We could lure it to one of our traps and fill it full of silver arrows. If we had silver arrows." Brogio's words were pointed. "I will take no chance that any of you come to harm. We need that silver."

His eyes turned to me, and I knew what I had to do.

EPISODE FIVE
Battle

I turned and sprinted through the woods. I knew not where to go, but felt the pull of her strength. My master had commanded that I capture Artemis' silver arrows, and the goddess knew his thoughts. Faster and faster. Through the woods into the open field with its circle of light. Artemis awaited. She shimmered and smiled at me.

"He has come for Brogio, for all of you." Her words were like slick oil oozing through my brain.

I slipped through the barrier from dark to light and bathed in the prickling caress of her glow.

"He hates him, you know. He still wants Selene."

Please, goddess. You know we need your silver arrows. There's no time!

She ignored my thoughts. "He can have sex with her now. Apollo is consumed with the thought of Brogio having sex with his virgin. She's been my virgin for this eternity." She smiled and shrugged. "My brother wants to stop them before they can be together."

Artemis, please help us. The silver arrows are all that will stop him now. I sat at her feet, tempted to lick her toes if that would help convince her of our need.

"Yes, that's true ... but, what's in it for me?" Her light turned a frosty shade of gray, and I oddly felt its icy sharpness.

If you don't give me the arrows, I will have to fight the were-jaguar. I knew I would be playing with fire if I angered her. *My bite might be the only thing that can kill him. Or ...*

She swirled in a black cloud around me. "No, I forbid you to put yourself at risk! You must obey me. We have an arrangement."

But, my Alpha and our pack will die if I cannot save them. I beg you. Please let me have your arrows.

Her light suddenly glowed golden, and she kneeled down next to me. "What will you give me in return?"

What do you want?

At that moment, she transformed into a silver husky in front of me, and I stared into her blue eyes as they pierced mine. She rubbed her head against my chest and then turned her hind quarters suggestively toward me. A seduction in exchange for Brogio's life.

*****

"My gods, the dog did it!" Kane pulled the quiver from my back and chuckled. "What'd you have to do to get this, dog?"

I responded with a growl. Brogio gently stroked my head. "I knew you could do it, Snow Blood! I'm sorry it had to come to that." He turned to Kane. "Come! Let's grab our bows from my nearby hunter's blind. We need to set up and attract the beast." He pointed to the edge of the woods where Selene was standing. "Snow Blood, guard Selene. You know the drill. Kane and I are off to battle."

Selene and I settled into a thick brush area. My keen hearing enabled me to alert to their footfalls. The creature heard them as well. Its roar sent a quick shiver up my spine. Selene wrapped her arms around me and pulled me closer. I could feel her heart pounding against my fur.

The creature's footsteps shook the ground as it followed Brogio and Kane's movements. A sickly smell permeated the air. Rotted meat and burnt fur overwhelmed my nose. Selene covered her mouth and gagged. Through the leaves, I spotted the were-jaguar. It was just ten feet from us. I dared not move with the embodiment of Apollo dangerously close. Suddenly, I remembered Kane's words that the were-jaguar would be able to hear Selene's pulse. I bolted from our hiding place, drawing the beast away from my master's love. It was a risky move leaving Selene alone, but a calculated one.

The beast screamed like a large cat and dashed after me. I could only be grateful Selene didn't scream and give away her hiding spot.

I ran through the trees as fast as I could. I felt the heat of its breath on my back. Despite its massive size, this beast was able to keep up with me.

155

Brogio taunted it – "What are you waiting for? I'm here!" I followed his voice, dodging the traps that awaited it.

Looking behind me, I saw the were-jaguar make one plunge forward. I leaped high in the air and sailed over a pit buried in the ground. I turned just to see the enraged were-jaguar fall through. Its scream shook the trees. I peered over the side and saw the beast twisting in agony on the sharp stakes.

Brogio and Kane were at the mouth of the opening before I could blink.

"This is going to hurt." Kane said. He grabbed an arrow from the quiver. "Damn the Gods," he screamed, releasing the first round into the monster. His hands began to blister as he reached for the second arrow and shot it off, aiming for the creature's head.

Brogio stood at the edge of the pit and gritted his teeth, but didn't scream. His hands blistered and smoldered as he loaded the bow and took deadly aim at the were-jaguar's brain. As he loaded the second silver arrow, his hands began to burn. Neither Brogio, nor Kane came prepared with gloves. The flesh from their hands started dripping off in chunks of liquid flame. Both Brogio and Kane screamed in agony. I remembered Brogio's conversation with Artemis about how silver burned vampire's skin. Deadly as well to the were-jaguar, Brogio and Kane released two more rounds of silver arrows into the monster. Its cries of agony mingled with those of both vampires as its wounds ignited with fire.

Again, my Alpha and his son released two more silver arrows from their burning hands.

The were-jaguar's screams formed words that gave us all pause. "Hades is coming for all of you! This is only the beginning of your troubles."

Its wounds smoldered as my male pack members shot two more silver arrows into it. "Damn it, I'm out," Kane yelled.

Brogio reached back into his quiver to discover he had only one remaining arrow. His fiery hand grabbed and loaded it, then sent it into the creature. The monster exploded into flames. A column of fire rose up and out of the pit. A flash of light burned my eyes as the fire exploded into ashes and fell to the ground.

Kane dropped his bow and pounded his scorched hands against nearby trees. He was trying to put out the flames of his burning hands. Brogio settled his bow across his chest where it wouldn't touch his skin. He whispered "ha-b'rakah" to each hand. Miraculously, the flames died upon the last syllable of the word. He walked to Kane and repeated the word. Kane dropped to the ground as the flames went out.

Brogio turned to me. "You should be with her." He furrowed his brow. He was displeased with me. "Go and protect Selene."

A tar-like form rose from the ashes. An acrid smell filled the air. Laughter shook the earth. Dark smoke circled me. It was so thick I couldn't see my Alpha. I couldn't see anything at all. I growled at the wall spinning around me. Then it rose up and flew away, almost like a bird!

"Great gods!" Kane shouted. "What was that?"

"Apollo," Brogio said quietly. "We haven't seen the last of him."

*****

"She is safe?" Brogio's eyes glowed red. His tone a dangerous question.

Yes.

"Where?"

I sprinted off with him in hot pursuit behind me.

Selene sprang from her hiding place and threw herself into Brogio's arms.

"You are safe!" He turned to me and smiled his appreciation.

Brogio pushed her back, examined her from head to toe. Selene appeared focused on his cinder-like hands.

"What has happened to you?" She gently pointed to the marred flesh.

"It's nothing." Kane interjected as he approached. "A good meal, and we'll be healed like new." His disappointment at her lack of concern for him spilled across his face. He watched closely as Selene ignored him and continued to examine Brogio's wounded appendages.

"Honestly, Selene, I'm going to be okay. Come everyone. Let's all go back to the house." Brogio turned and pulled Selene to his side, wincing from the pain of his injured hands. "It's obvious that Apollo will find us no matter where we go. We need to recuperate and prepare for whatever comes next."

* * * * *

I spent the next several days watching the repairs on the house while my pack slept. I kept a keen eye on our surroundings. How Brogio managed to have the manpower that he did amazed me. A hundred workers spread throughout the house replacing windows, repairing the damaged roof, and cleaning up dead crows.

My forages in the forest were satisfying and uneventful, except for the recurring scent of ... other dogs? No, wolves. Many of them. Their fresh droppings and the pungent, repulsive smell of recent kills piqued my curiosity about them. I pushed down a passing urge to seek them out. It would only result in the wolf pack Alpha feeling threatened and challenging me. He would be no match for me, and I had no desire to harm a member of my own species.

The fifth night in our new location, Brogio and Kane drank blood from crystal wine glasses. Selene dined on a large salad. Her laughter filled the house. All appeared well, so I decided to take a turn around the perimeter of the property. As I reached the woods, a cold fog crept through the trees and rolled toward the outside of the house. The hairs stood up on my back at the steady purpose of the dense, gray fog. Its rotten smell prickled my nose. I knew instantly what it carried.

I rushed back to the house, hit the slightly open door and skidded to an abrupt stop. Lucky that I skid, or I would have run straight into Brogio.

"What the..."

Bringer of death! My mind screamed into his.

It menacingly oozed between our legs and spread along the floor of the house. First the entry, then the den, then the dining room. Selene's laughter turned to a cough ending in a chocking sound.

"Brogio! Quick! Selene!" Kane's voice rang through the house.

We rushed to the dining room. Kane cradled an unconscious Selene in his arms. Panic spread across his face. "She's collapsed!"

The creeping fog surrounded each of us with no effect. I growled as it slithered across the floor and crossed to a slightly opened window and slid out into the night.

Brogio rushed to Selene. He placed three fingers on her neck. "No pulse." He bit his wrist, opened her mouth and tried to force his blood down her. Pulling her to him, he sat down in a dining room chair balancing her on his lap and watched her closely. Minutes went by, and she stirred and breathed out. Relief spread across his face as he found her pulse. "She lives!"

I went over to my Alpha and sat next to him. Minutes ticked by. Kane took a step toward Brogio. "But, she's not come around."

Brogio touched Selene's cheek gently. "Wake up, my love! Let my blood heal you."

More minutes passed. Kane moved closer and put his hand on Brogio's shoulder. "It's not working."

Brogio stood, the despair on his face made me heart sick. He ran toward the stairs carrying her up, taking two at a time. He shouted over his shoulder, "Kane, get a doctor! She's not responding to anything. We have to try anything we can!"

*****

She was as pale as the silver of her hair. It spread around her shoulders and arms, and I thought she looked void of life, like one of the marble statues that adorned either side of Brogio's entrance gates.

Kane had gone at his break-neck speed to the emergency room of the hospital. He used the vampire ability to compel one of the doctors just coming off duty to return to the house with him. Dr. Williams was a man who looked to be in his early forties. The green surgical scrubs he was wearing stretched over a tall, thin body. Though his face was still young, his brown hair was turning prematurely gray. His concern for Selene spilled across his face as he examined her. "We need to get her to a hospital for blood tests, and into intensive care."

"Not unless I or my ... dog can be with her at all times." Brogio searched the eyes of the physician.

The doctor raised his eyebrows in surprise. "That's impossible! Dogs aren't allowed in intensive care, let alone the hospital!"

"Then draw her blood now, Dr. Williams, and get it tested. I won't leave her alone."

"As you wish." The doctor's reply sounded curt. "But I don't know if she'll make it through the night without complete medical care. And even then, I'm not sure she will pull through in her condition." The stoic physician drew several tubes of blood, labeled, and placed them in his bag. Straightening, he turned to Brogio. "I will do what I can, but I won't be able to return until later tomorrow morning."

Brogio stared deeply into the physician's eyes, compelling him to obey. "Send a nurse with the necessary supplies and medicines from the hospital within the hour. You will do so without question. You will rush the blood tests at the laboratory and return here personally with the results by three o'clock this morning. Do you understand?"

The doctor appeared to be in a daze. He nodded obediently and rushed out to his car.

At that moment, I wondered if I would be able to compel a human being to do my bidding as Brogio did. Since I couldn't speak, I doubted I would be able to make my commands clear. I was however willing to try.

*****

Selene was not improving. Nothing seemed to work. The nurse came and set up IV bags and put her on oxygen. She tried to make Selene comfortable. The doctor returned to say the quick analysis of the blood tests were not definitive. The symptoms were plague-like.

"We must quarantine her!" He handed a medical mask to the nurse, Brogio, and Kane.

The nurse adjusted hers while Brogio and Kane set theirs aside on a nearby antique dresser.

"The rest of you need to be tested and isolated!" Dr. Williams' voice betrayed his fear of what Selene might have.

Again, Brogio locked onto the doctor's eyes. "No, doctor. It is all right. You will think no more along these lines. None of us here share her symptoms. You are merely treating one sick patient."

The doctor shook his head, packed up his bag, and provided the nurse with specific instructions. "Keep the drip going. We don't want her to get dehydrated. Continue the oxygen and in case of infection, the doxycycline every four hours. "Call me if there is a change."

Before he left, Brogio stared deeply into the doctor's eyes again. "You will speak of this to no one. You will not reveal that you have seen this patient, ever. Do you understand?"

The doctor nodded his head in agreement as Brogio pressed a thick stack of cash into the physician's hand.

Over the next day, I sat by guarding Selene. Brogio had also kept vigilant at night, but he had to go to his rest at sunrise. Selene looked so fragile, hooked up to IVs, oxygen, and a heart-lung monitor. The machine made quite a bit of noise with its steady beeping.

Nurse Julie administered the medicine that the doctor had left. She worked without sleep, having been compelled by my Alpha. Her middle-aged face revealed her exhaustion. Small and efficient, her smooth movements around Selene lulled me into dozing by the bed, waking every few hours to see if Selene had improved. There was no change.

At sunset that night, Brogio quickly returned to sit beside Selene, never taking his eyes from her. He seemed helpless in this situation, despite all of the magic that he had exhibited since I had met him.

Hours later, Kane, who had been surprisingly absent, returned, and stood by Brogio. "I have been using your computer in your office doing some checking." He placed a large hand on his maker's shoulder.

Brogio's eyes never left Selene.

"Apollo is the healer of the gods, but he is also the bringer of disease and death. He has the ability to send plague."

Brogio finally turned to look at his progeny. "Why would he want to kill Selene? From what Artemis has told Snow Blood, Apollo wants her for himself."

"Perhaps he sent it thinking it would kill us. Or, maybe we are somehow immune and she isn't?"

I moved closer to the bed to watch Selene. For hours she appeared corpse-like and eerily still. Now, suddenly, she started thrashing around on the bed, crying out, "Leave me alone! Leave me!" At one point, she sat straight up, gasped for air, and fell backward onto her pillow. Then, again, she bolted straight up in the bed.

I tried to climb onto the bed to comfort her, but Brogio pushed me away in his attempt to prevent her from falling out of the bed. Kane, knowing he should not interfere, took a step back, his eyes filled with surprise. Nurse Julie ran to help Brogio steady her patient. Together they gently laid her back down. She kept silent the rest of the night.

Brogio and Kane left at daybreak. I gently crawled up on the bed, close to Selene's face, carefully avoiding the tubes and wires attached to the equipment. I watched her even more intently. The thrashing didn't return. That day, her fever increased, and the nurse applied cold towels to her arms, legs and forehead. Late in the afternoon, her fever broke.

Brogio and Kane returned at sunset. "My gods, her cheeks have some renewed color!" Brogio flew to her side. Kane went to the other side of the bed, and I jumped down, heading for the front door so that I could relieve myself outside.

When I returned, I found them helping her to sit up. I hopped back up on the bed to her side and pushed my nose under her hand. She squeezed my head briefly. My heart leaped for joy!

Brogio sat her up even more, offering her a glass of water to sip.

Brogio turned to the nurse, his eyes full of questions.

"I have no idea, sir. Her fever spiked earlier, and then it broke. It was nothing I did." The nurse shrugged and took the glass to fill it with more water in the adjoining bathroom for her patient.

"How do you feel, my love?" Brogio pulled her close and kissed her forehead.

"It's all such a blur ... I ..." She sat back and sighed. "What happened to me?"

"You've been ill and unconscious for several days." Kane touched Selene's pale hand, but Brogio stopped him with a withering stare. Kane smiled and sat in a chair next to the bed.

"Dreams ... I had such strange dreams." Selene murmured. I drew closer to hear her.

"A beautiful woman, surrounded by ever-changing light. Swirling in my dreams. Her words confusing. She said that her brother's cunning plan had backfired." She took the glass from the nurse and sipped the water.

"Leave us!" Brogio commanded.

"But, sir, I must attend to my patient. The doctor will want . . ."

Brogio stood up and turned to the nurse. "You have worked without stopping. I thank you for your constant care. Now, please go to the kitchen and make yourself something to eat. There is ample food for you in the refrigerator. It's down the stairs and through the den and dining room. There will be ample time to examine her later."

Nurse Julie reluctantly left the room. Brogio turned back to Selene's side.

"Laughter, her laughter ... and a male voice, yelling ... She called him 'Apollo'." Selene gulped out in-between sips of water.

"Tell us." Kane leaned forward.

"It was like she was laughing at him, and he was angry."

"Who? Artemis and Apollo?" Kane whispered.

"Quiet, Kane! Let her tell it in her own way." Brogio moved closer to Selene. "Go on."

"She said something about how his blunders gave her pleasure. She goaded him about his frustration."

"Ah, so we were correct. He made a mistake with his plague." Kane sat back in his chair and stretched out his legs.

Selene continued. "She asked how his purifying ceremony to ward off the evil was going. He kept yelling at her to be quiet. Then, it seemed as if he pushed her away."

"Did he say anything else, Selene?" Brogio took her hand.

Normally Selene would avert her eyes, not look at him. But this time she stared him full-on in the eyes.

"Please, Selene, whatever you tell us might be important." Brogio kissed her hand.

She then surprised us by pulling back the bed sheets and moving her legs to the side of the bed. "Yes, knowledge is indeed power." Her stature seemed to grow before my eyes. "He wants me for himself." She steadied herself as she stood up next to the bed, her chin raised, her eyes full of pride. "He begged me to forgive him."

Brogio sat straight up. Kane leaned forward again and whispered, "Really?"

"Yes." She took a tentative step and then faced us all. "Women are his weakness. He can't resist. He confessed that he sent the plague to kill everyone but me. He makes rash decisions. He promised me life instead of darkness."

Brogio stood and towered over her, but she didn't back away from him. "And, how do you feel about that?" His eyes never left hers.

"I would rather be dead." She took his hand. "Don't you see, Brogio? We have a weapon against him now, and we will use it."

*****

Selene sat by the window. The healthy glow of her cheeks displayed her recovery. Nurse Julie told us that

Selene's rapid improvement was nothing less than miraculous as she left the night before. I lay with my head on her legs as she hummed a cheerful tune. No longer tentative and unsure, she exuded a strength that only women who know their power over men can wield.

The sun would set soon. I napped and fell into a deep sleep filled with strange dreams of my own.

Two men, one golden and the other dark bathed in a red glow, argued.

"We had a deal, Hades!" The golden one was unusually handsome with broad shoulders and golden curls that framed the strong features of his face.

"Then keep your sister away from Persephone!" The dark one was sinister, red eyes glowed in a black face. He reeked of sulfur. It baffled me that I could smell him in my dream!

"I don't control Artemis! What about my son? And, you agreed to help me bring these vamps back to your domain."

"Asclepius will have to fend for himself! No one threatens my wife!"

"I thought my son's restoration of people to life was reducing your dominion's numbers!"

"Never mind that! I can't live without Persephone! That bitch sister of yours threatens even now to lure her away from me! Get rid of these blood suckers on your own, and I will still take possession of their souls in my world!"

"We made a deal!" Apollo's frustration seemed to shake my dream but was drowned out by Artemis' gusty laughter.

I awoke abruptly and stared into Selene's questioning eyes. Shaking from head to tail, I yawned and pondered my strange dream. Was it a message from Artemis? What did it all mean? I couldn't wait to share this with Brogio so that we could try and decipher this.

It was late afternoon. The sun invaded the windows of Selene's bedroom. Its intensity grew and spread to every corner of the room. The heat became too unbearable to remain on the window seat. Selene and I jumped away from the spot where we had wasted away the day listening to music.

The house shook and rumbled like the sound of a freight train pounding down on us. The sun became larger and brighter. Fire consumed the woods outside. With no time to spare, Selene sprang into action.

"Quick, Snow! It's Apollo, he's coming! We have to wake Brogio!"

We sprang down the stairs. The paintings on the walls crashed behind us. We ran to the front door and Selene swung it open. The heat hit us like a blast furnace. We just cleared the house before it burst into flames! We made a dash for the winery cellar door. Selene's skin began to blister. The fur on my back burst into flames, but Selene grabbed a blue painter's tarp near the door and beat out the flames, burning her hands. She cried out. I pushed her to the door, and we fell inside and went down into the darkness.

The coolness of the wine cellar gave momentary relief. Selene finished beating out the rest of the flames on my back with the tarp. Pain shot through me like thousands of daggers. Her pale skin and hands were in ruins. I tried to lick her hands, but she screamed in agony.

Brogio and Kane were at her side before I could call them.

The sun! Everything is on fire!

Brogio ignored my words and examined Selene's burns. "My gods! They've hurt you, my love. I will avenge this."

"We can help her, but we first have to escape the fire!" Kane searched the cellar boundaries.

"There's a way out underground." Brogio pointed to a small passageway. "An escape route."

You can't go into the light! All of us will burn! I ran along to the passageway and sniffed it out.

"It goes deeper into the ground." Brogio still was inspecting Selene's burned skin and hair.

Kane grabbed me. "You are burned badly, dog, but you will heal with some human blood."

My pain subsided to the background as panic overtook all my other senses.

"Come." Brogio gently pushed Selene forward. "Our only hope is to go deeper underground."

Brogio took the lead. Selene staggered along with me behind her and Kane taking up the rear. Deeper and deeper we went in the blackness, but the freight-train rumble became more intense. Crouching in the dark dampness, we waited. Minutes passed and then the rumble subsided. I could only imagine the house, the winery, the forest, everything around us burned to the ground. Selene's small whimpers of pain were the only sound.

"It had to be Apollo, father." Kane's voice broke through the dark. "He drove his sun chariot close to earth to kill us all."

"Yes, and in his careless rage, he has again made Selene his victim." I could hear my Alpha draw her closer to him as she cried out in pain.

As he bit into his vein, I was reminded of my old human Alpha biting into an apple. I heard Brogio whisper, "Drink, my love. It will heal you."

I could hear her sobbing as she sucked from his wrist.

I tried to lick my wounds but couldn't reach them. Kane bent down and pulled me close, licking the burns on my back. The burning pain subsided, and I could feel the rough patches knitting together and my skin instantly healing.

You can heal with your tongue?

Kane stared at me, bewildered.

Brogio answered, "At great cost to himself, yes. He's rather stingy with the ability."

Kane eyed me. "Be still, my dog brother."

It was in that moment that Kane truly became my litter mate. I knew that henceforth I would die to save the three with whom I crouched in a corner in the dark. It no longer mattered that I had been torn from a life I had loved. Circumstances had dealt me this fate, and these three cared for me whenever it counted.

Brogio intuitively knew when the sun had left the sky. After a while, he led the way as Selene and Kane climbed up the iron ladder that led to the surface. I tried but found it hard to navigate, so I just leaped from the ground up to where the others stood. No problem.

For as far as we could see, everything was gone. The forest, the house, and winery. There was little hope that anyone, or anything nearby had survived. I felt a deepening sadness for all those who had died so needlessly at the whim of Apollo.

*****

Chunks of embers and small fires still burned. We walked back to where the house and winery had been. Nothing remained; the wooden parts of the house and wine cellar were ashes. The stone had melted. The surrounding forest, all the animals, everything had been devastated. I felt numb. I hopped along - the ground was still hot and burned the pads of my feet. Kane lifted me onto his back, and I perched upon his shoulders feeling loved and protected.

Selene's beautiful skin and hair had begun to heal. Brogio's blood had restored her face and arms to resemble raw-looking sunburn. Her usually silky hair still was dry and straw-like, singed in places. My burns would remain until I could find human blood. Though they were much better from Kane's healing tongue.

Brogio stepped over to what had been the estate driveway. He appeared to be communicating with someone as he closed his eyes and put his fingers to his temples.

Afterward, he returned to Selene, lifted her in his arms, and we made our way into the nearby destroyed town that had once been Kelowna.

"It's gone!" Selene cried out in despair. "What will we do?"

Brogio sat her down. "Don't fear. Someone is on the way to get us now."

Kane lifted me higher on his back and sighed. "Your network of resources never ceases to amaze me."

Brogio sighed. "One of the few advantages of living for thousands of years." Brogio turned a distraught face to his progeny. "The heartbreak is losing those that matter most. My men here are lost."

My Alpha's strength, and that of his son, was amazing. After walking for miles, each carrying Selene and me, they decided to sprint to the next town over. Neither Selene, nor I, appeared to be a burden to either of them. They carried us through the night, alternating between sprinting and walking to avoid aggravating Selene's still-raw skin.

Before sunrise, a long black stretch limousine pulled up beside us on the road from Kelowna. The doors opened automatically, and two men jumped out to assist everyone inside the car.

Kane sat in the front seat and immediately asked the driver, "What are the reports of what happened here?"

The driver looked to Brogio. My Alpha nodded once, tightening his grip on Selene who collapsed against him in exhaustion.

"Some sort of catastrophic coastal event ... They are saying that it could've been caused by an inner solar system flyby of our dual Sun."

"Dual sun?" Kane leaned forward.

"Something about a mini-solar system entering ours."

"Do tell." Kane sat back and took a deep breath. "And the damage?"

"The west coast of Canada and parts of Washington and Oregon were taken out. Don't know about anywhere else." The driver sighed.

I searched Brogio's face for his reaction. His sorrow spread across the vampire's face, and his shoulders slumped from the weight of what had happened. Yet, I didn't blame him for this. It only added to my resentment of Apollo and Artemis and their vain attempts to manipulate all of us.

"Thank the gods for Master's deep wine cellars and underground garages!" Kane let out a deep sigh. "We would've been toast."

We drove through the night and the next day, only stopping to refuel with the additional fuel stored in the large car trunk and make pit stops. I was thankful Brogio had summoned a car instead of trying to transport us by other means. Selene and my injuries would have made anything else too uncomfortable. The car's blacked-out windows allowed my Alpha and brother to sleep away from the bright sun. During the night, I watched the miles fly by us, spanning a path of destruction. The car's mini-fridge was well-stocked with human blood, and I lapped at a bowl the relief driver provided for me every few hours. The burns on my back healed quickly. My fur filled in where the empty patches had been. Selene slowly transformed, her pale skin flawless; her silver hair like a moonbeam. The small mini-fridge also held small fruit and other finger foods to sustain her, which the drivers restocked as soon as we reached unaffected areas. Brogio slept with his arm hung loosely around her, while a comatose Kane held onto one of my hind legs throughout the days that followed.

Just before the fourth nightfall, the landscape changed. Agricultural, dairy farms, and apple orchards lined the roads in lush greens.

Brogio awoke as day became night. "How close to Gaspereau, Anton?"

"Another few miles, master. Then your estate near Wolfville." Anton's reply was prompt and respectful.

"Gaspereau? Your Nova Scotia winery?" Kane sat bolt upright and let go of my leg. "Another replica of British Columbia and Oregon, I would imagine!"

176

Brogio smiled, then hugged Selene closer to him as she continued to sleep.

I wondered how long it would be before Apollo launched another attack and shattered this momentary tranquility.

*****

Wolfville Winery proved to be yet another replica of Oregon. It made new surroundings easy to acclimate. The days moved from fall to winter. Kane and I patrolled the outer perimeter of the property, learning every nook and hollow in the surrounding woods. Brogio, on the other hand, seemed to want only to explore the depths of Selene's eyes. His passion for her grew in its intensity, and Selene returned it in kind. Kane and I often interrupted their passionate embraces in the den, the kitchen, and even on the stairs. It became embarrassing, even awkward.

On one such occasion, Kane blurted, "Oh, why don't the two of you get it over with!" The smirk on his face made them both burst into laughter. "It's not like we'll be around for much longer once Apollo attacks again."

The pair shrugged and descended the stairs. I wasn't sure what held them back from mating. But the need in the air was so thick I could have chewed it in half with my fangs.

The next three weeks were spent hunting, preparing more pits and traps in the woods for another attack, and watching more of the same between my Alpha and his chosen mate. And then, the visions started.

At first they came to me in dreams. Soon they interrupted my days. Soldiers, thousands of soldiers marching on the estate across a snowy field. The golden one, dressed in gold armor, led them driving a chariot pulled by two perfectly matched grey horses, gold flames shooting from their heads. The faces, arms, and legs of the soldiers were golden, like the metal of their armor. They moved in unison, never missing a step, lances held upward and slightly pointing forward. At first, I could just see a brief glimpse of them. As the dreams progressed, more and more of it was revealed. Apollo was coming for us.

I met Brogio in his resting place in the wine cellar as he rose from his sleep the next night. *He is coming, my Alpha.*

"Yes, I have had the dreams as well." He turned to Kane who joined us just outside their resting place. "Let's make final preparations. Our respite is over. He approaches."

What do you plan, Brogio? I knew we had laid the same type of traps in the forest as we had at the previous estate, but Brogio and Kane seemed to have something else in mind.

"Soon, Snow Blood. Soon you will see." He walked away leaving me to wonder.

*****

The next night, vampires came in droves. First Leander, who was greeted warmly by his maker in the entranceway of the house.

"Father, you honor us to fight for you." Leander was a handsome blonde man, as fair as Kane appeared dark and sinister. "My coven will arrive shortly."

Brogio turned to me with his arm around Leander's shoulder. "Snow Blood, this is Leander. He is my second eldest child. All of the vampires I have made control their own covens. Leander, Snow Blood is my youngest."

Leander saluted me as he stared curiously at Brogio.

"It's a long story." Brogio then changed the subject as he leaned in to his progeny. "How many, Leander?"

"With mine, that of Ian, Leslie, Joseph, and Alexander, at least one thousand."

Who are those that Leander names, Brogio?

"My progeny, vampires of my making and your brethren," Brogio shot back to my mind.

A thousand vampires here? The thought was mind-boggling!

"Excellent, Leander. Thank you, my son. Now, come, take some wine with me or blood, if you wish, after your journey."

The vampires began to arrive at midnight. First Ian and Leslie, then Joseph and Alexander arrived. Ian was tall with long dark hair and a slender body. Unlike his maker, he was dressed all in red. His green eyes surveyed the room and landed on me with a smile. Leslie was a beautiful, tiny woman with black hair and eyes. Her wide smile made dimples on her brown skin. She was dressed in black leather and tall stilettos. She and Ian seemed to be mated. Joseph looked no older than a teenager, and, like Kane, he was full of mischief. Alexander was almost as tall as our Alpha. His broad shoulders and red hair seemed to fill the room. I liked each of them instantly.

The clock over the fireplace mantle struck one o'clock in the morning. The sound of a thousand bats flew around and through the estate, settling in the trees surrounding the house and winery.

They aren't in human form? I asked Brogio in my head.

"Better for them to take the shape of the night creatures to guard against intruders." Brogio let his eyes settle on mine and mentally replied.

But where will they go during the day? Who will guard against a day attack?

"In this place many years ago, I built miles of underground tunnels and alcoves. They will rest there during the day." He silently responded. Then, he and Leander raised their wine glasses with their compatriots and took long sips of blood.

In that moment, realization struck me. I raised my concern to Brogio. *You and the rest of your considerable pack will be defenseless during the daylight.*

His words crept into my mind. "A problem not yet resolved." He turned to make plans with his other children and introduced them to Selene who appeared fascinated by them. It was one massive family reunion of sorts.

I sought solace in the forest, looking for a solution. Could I be a maker? Would it be possible for me before another attack to find a wild pack and make them my coven, with my daylight attributes? It was far-fetched, but I had to try. If Brogio was in need of the help of a thousand vampires to offset the power of Apollo, I wanted to aid his effort.

In the three weeks since our arrival at Wolfville, when tracking to quench my blood thirst, I caught the scent of wolves. They always kept out of sight, apparently afraid of me and my demon smell. I put my nose to the ground, took in the aroma of earth, moss, leaves, tree roots, rabbit, squirrel, bird and ... wait ... wolf. I locked onto the smell, let my keen nose follow only the wolf trail that led to droppings, kill sites and mating rituals. I paused only to sniff the air for any clues I might have missed.

One encounter led me astray. I came upon a large doe that bolted at the sight of me. She gave me a merry chase weaving in and out of the trees, and over fallen logs. Small creatures scattered as we passed. Squirrels scampered up tree trunks. A rabbit darted across my path, and I barely missed it. An owl hooted at me from above. I considered it a fun distraction and didn't make an effort to try and take the doe. An attempt, perhaps, to avoid the possibility of becoming a pack-master? The doe darted ahead of me and out into a clearing that had the vague familiarity of the open field where I had encountered Artemis at our past two homes. I braced myself for contact with the goddess, but she did not appear. Had the doe led me there to make me think about Artemis? Skidding to a stop, I watched the doe disappear into the woods on the other side of the field. The

181

moon sunk lower in the sky, and I realized I was wasting time. Shaking my entire body from head to toe, I refocused on my primary task and followed my nose. I followed back the way I had come, through the fallen leaves and branches. Finally, I recaptured the early scent of the wolf pack. They had made a recent kill. The blood trail led me deeper into the woods to a small clearing near a cave. Success! Six healthy, and more importantly, well-fed wolves gathered around a deer kill.

I lifted my head to the moon, then let out a howl as I turned from dog to demon.

The pack snarled at me in unison. Two gulped down a few pieces of deer meat. Four challenged me, ears flat, fangs dripping with blood, hackles raised. To them, I was an intruder wanting to steal their captured prey. To me, they were a fearless pack that when changed over would give Apollo another challenge to fight off.

But first, they needed to prove themselves worthy.

Four wolves spread-out in front of their deer meal, while a fifth scrawny one stole away, dragging part of the kill to a stand of trees twenty feet away. No intruder was going to interrupt his meal.

Silence. Wind blew in the trees. A large black wolf moved in front of the other four, poised in an eternal crouch, frozen before me with a permanent snarl.

The black wolf sprang at me with the other four leaping behind him. All five tried to take me down at once. Claws ripped, teeth snapped. I was determined not to bite them in case my venom was poison to them. I spun in a tight circle, slashing at them with my claws. I outsized them and grabbed one by the throat, tossing him against a nearby tree. Spinning again, I slashed one across the face with both my claws, and he yelped and fell. The other two backed off a bit at the sight of their injured pack members. The black wolf came at me from the side and sprang, trying to slash my throat. I stood up on my hind legs, and he broadsided me, then fell to the ground. I staggered back, then pounced in his direction as he jumped back on his feet. I hit him head on, and we tumbled in the dirt, rolling hard into a tree trunk. We both jumped to our feet, but I slashed open his shoulder. He yelped and fell.

The other four were on me from behind immediately. I spun and with my claws and body knocked them all to the ground. I took the one I had thrown into a tree earlier and ripped out his throat with my claws, throwing him with a thud against another tree. The one with the slashed face tried to fight but was too weak from loss of blood. I slashed his face again with my front claws. He dropped to the ground in a heap.

The other two knocked into me, tearing at my shoulders and chest with their teeth. I clawed, pushing them away. I leaped onto the one closest to me and broke its neck by landing with all my weight onto it. It lay motionless on the ground, still breathing. The other one staggered to his feet. I hit him in the neck and buried my claws into him. He fell over and rolled on the frozen ground, wincing in pain.

I heard a growl behind me. The sixth wolf that had been too busy eating to join the fight approached me cautiously.

He was small and wide. Nothing like the lean tall fighters that tumbled with me. Yet the others had conceded to the scrawny one. I was puzzled by this.

Scrawny assessed me with a cunning intelligence that sent shivers down to my tail. My heightened vampire senses allowed me to read this creature's intent. Even as I stood in my intimidating demon form, he did not blink, did not balk. Instead, he huffed and sat down on his hind legs.

The gesture was demeaning. In one action he had said I wasn't worth the trouble. He would soon learn that this was not an appropriate language to address his Alpha.

Scrawny was ten feet away when I charged him. He leaped to meet me half way. He met me scrape for scrape. He went for my throat. I pulled back and covered his muzzle like he was an adolescent pup with my massive jaw. He yelped and managed to pull away. His anger only grew, and he tried clawing at my eyes.

I ran him into a tree opening a huge gash in his side. He yelped, but the fighting went on. He jumped up and attacked my hind quarters. I howled at the fangs digging in on the soft part of my leg. I turned to free myself, and he smiled up at me, letting go of my leg. Our eye contact was his signal to pounce on my back. He positioned his head to go directly for my throat. Our jaws snapped at each other, but I continued to avoid biting. This put me at a huge disadvantage. He bit into my back, puncturing the skin. I swirled around, flinging him off and swiping a huge gash across his back. The blood oozed from him. He had lost a lot of blood. He let go and staggered back. He shook his head side-to-side and sat down, dazed.

I sprinted to the wolf that lay with his backside curled the wrong way around a trunk. This was the one whose throat I had ripped open with my paws. Lifeless, almost all of the blood in his body was gone. I too was bleeding from enough places to quickly force my blood down his open mouth.

The blood oozed into him. I hoped that my blood was enough to turn him.

Scrawny fell on his side from his sitting position. I rushed to him as he lay convulsing in the throes of his death. I let the blood drip from my wounds into his mouth.

In turn, I went to each wolf, each one was lifeless, bled out as I had hoped. I dripped my blood into each of their mouths.

Six once vital wolves lay on the ground lifeless. For what seemed like a moon's cycle, I waited. I struggled with my injuries as I returned to dog form. Bleeding from my back, shoulders, chest, my hind legs, my face and front paws, I tried to lick at each one, hoping my blood would turn this wolf pack into my coven of followers.

Scrawny lay not far from me. I noticed that his right front paw twitched, and I moved to sit next to him. His muzzle spasmed. Red flashing eyes pierced me with hate. The real battle started before I realized that my plan had worked.

The scrawny one had no plans to be subservient to me as a wolf, or as a demon. He lunged at my leg immediately. I was faster. Even in my wounded state, I body blocked him, knocking him on his back and pinning him by the neck. He struggled, using claws to push me, wiggling his body to try to get free.

I held him steady as his soul attached itself to me. I was master, he the child. Yet he fought. I growled. *Stop it.*

Scrawny paused in his fight to be free. Five more souls hooked themselves one by one as I clamped down on my child's throat. Their lives felt like bloated water bags hanging from my heart.

Is this how Brogio feels? I wondered to myself.

"You get used to the weight." Brogio's voice rang out in my head.

How my master found me, I didn't know. He stood nearby leaning against a tree watching me try to tame the scrawny one.

Brogio chuckled. "You should know by now there is nothing you do that I don't know about."

Scrawny squirmed, and I pressed my claws down into his throat. *Be still,* I commanded.

"Your first child. "Brogio beamed with pride. "He's feisty."

Okay, any suggestions on how to handle him?

"Yeah. Let him go."

I unclenched my teeth and pulled back with my claws, Scrawny immediately sprang up and sprinted into the nearby trees.

"No, Snow Blood." Brogio held me back by the scruff of my neck. "Let him go. Let them all go."

My emotions swirled at being bound to six souls' every thought. I had always liked being alone, aside from my domesticated days when I felt responsible for little Tommy. Now, I never would be. Even Scrawny's thoughts invaded me. His hurt. His broken pride. The other five crept closer to me. Lying down near me, they spread their front legs out in front of them, almost in unison, and rested their heads on their legs. They closed their eyes and waited, and I felt their acceptance and devotion.

Is this what happens when you create vampire children?

"Yes." Brogio's thoughts crept back at me. "Acceptance is normally immediate. You are their master now."

But what of the Scrawny one? Why does he resist?

"Only the strongest of wills can." Brogio spoke to me aloud. "He will come around in time."

The realization of what had happened, the wounds I had sustained in the fight, and the loss of blood weakened me. I staggered toward Brogio who was watching nearby. Suddenly, I felt my Alpha's arms around me, raising me up, and pouring his blood from his opened wrist into my mouth. Pure pleasure rushed through me. My intense pain ceased. Then total blackness.

When I awoke, I remained on the cold, blood-soaked ground where I had created my coven. I felt refreshed and satisfied. Brogio stood above me, watching closely as he licked closed the wrist he had opened to heal me. My new wolf coven crowded around, and my mind was filled with their voices. *I will serve you, Alpha. Give us your commands. How can. . .*

"Enough!" Brogio's voice broke through the clutter, commanding them to silence. "Do not speak until Snow Blood commands it! You'll fry his mind with your incessant questions!"

My pack pulled in closer to me and snarled.

We don't take orders from you.

Enough. I stood to lick my master's hand. The transformation of my coven seemed complete. My mind raced with ideas for our part in the oncoming battle. But one kernel of an idea implanted inside my brain. *If Apollo takes human form true to my dream, perhaps I could take him down with my venom, hopefully with all of our venom.*

Brogio cautioned. "Only as a last resort. He is more dangerous than you know."

Kneeling down, he held out a red leather collar with silver spikes. "You are a brave creature, Snow Blood. Your loyalty means a great deal to me. You risked it all to create daytime protection for all of us. With luck, you will have shared your tolerance for light with them. Let this collar signify that you are henceforth the leader of your own coven." He placed the collar around my neck. I lowered my neck to humbly accept it.

Brogio disappeared with the first rays of sunlight from the clearing in the forest. I stood to face my wolves, who had formed a circle around me. Soon, I would know if I had sentenced them to a fiery death, or a blood-filled eternity. Neither would be easy for me to face. Now healed from their fatal wounds, my wolves paced restlessly around me, anticipating whatever would come next. They knew without my intending them, that I awaited what fate the sunrise would bring them. Novice at mind linking with them, I let slip my worry and anticipation about the sun. A pink glow spread across the sky, streaked with blue and gold. It was beautiful. The sun appeared and spread through the trees into the clearing. I closed my eyes as it spread across my face. It slowly reached out and licked the bodies of my progeny, soon covering them completely. They live! They are day walkers! I threw back my head and howled at the sun. Their voices joined me. Relief spread through all of us as the sun lit the day with promise.

We raced out into the woods and hunted. I watched with pride as my young neophytes trapped and awkwardly attacked their prey. It was a blood bath at first. Their inclination was to tear apart their prey. I soon illustrated what my Alpha had taught me. They caught on quickly and made me proud. I could feel Scrawny trailing us. Not joining, but ever watchful. I hoped I could win him over.

I wondered what to call each one of my children, but that would have to come later. Guarding my Alpha and his family became all-consuming this day.

I spent hours positioning my coven throughout the estate to stand guard. I would know the instant we were being attacked. The long day dwindled into night. I had just led my day walkers into the house to meet the others who were waiting for us in the den with Brogio, Kane, and Selene when the pounding of heavy footsteps outside alerted me. I ran down to the gates of the estate. This would give Brogio an advanced glimpse through my eyes. Hordes of them approached from more than one thousand yards away. They appeared in person as they had in my dream, marching through the snow-covered field. Only now, each soldier stood more than seven-feet-tall, flanked by twin were-jaguars that towered over them. Out front, what had to be the golden-god Apollo grew to be the tallest of what looked to be several thousand soldiers. I scampered back to the house to defend with the others.

Back in the den, everyone stood in expectation. My coven crouched on the floor, wary of the others. Brogio questioned aloud, "Why in the world would he take human form?"

"He wants me to see how beautiful, how irresistible he is." Selene stood next to Brogio, tall and smiling knowingly. "He doesn't want me to see him as a monster. There's no allure in that."

Kane snorted. "Why would he come at night when we are strongest? He has little advantage in that."

Brogio walked over to Kane and placed his hand on his son's arm. "His pride is such that he'd want to prove he can beat me on my own turf, during my own time." Brogio returned to his love and took her arm. "Come, Selene. I have a safe room that will give you protection."

She pulled her arm free. "No, Brogio, I will stand with you." She stood up so tall that she almost reached his chin.

"You can't. What if you are harmed ... or worse, killed or captured?" He searched her eyes.

"You know I am right! I can bring advantage if he sees me with you!"

"I'm not sure what you mean?" Brogio scratched at his brow.

"If you saw me with him, would it not rattle you?" She smiled and winked. "Let's try and catch him off guard." Her confidence radiated. "Besides, if you are killed, I would rather die with my friends than spend eternity with that ... selfish bastard."

My Alpha knew she was right. If he experienced the true death, Selene's being a slave to Apollo would be a worse fate.

*****

We gathered in front of the house. A thousand, or more, of the various covens in bat-form had arisen from sleep and filled the surrounding trees. Brogio commanded the first wave of our defense. All his coven leaders flanked him and stood at attention. So too did my coven of wolves, minus Scrawny, who waited impatiently behind us from afar.

Apollo and his army crashed through the gates of the estate and began the 500 yard march to the house.

191

Nodding slightly, Brogio signaled to his vampire children, Ian, then Leslie, Joseph, Alexander and Kane, who had all shed their clothing. I wondered how they would fight these armored soldiers. Their voices screamed "ATTACK" as they each morphed into demon warriors.

Ian became an upright warrior dressed in red armor covering his arms and head. A bird-like beak and horns protruded from his helmet. He stood eight-feet tall on cloven feet. His talons held a long scythe.

Leslie joined him. Spikes sprouted from her shoulders. Horns grew out and pointed upward from her now skeleton face. Her muscled arms grew longer than the length of her body, and her muscular chest bulged with power. She matched Ian's height. She carried a six-foot-long maul large enough to crush a man's head.

Joseph's head took the shape of a ram with four horns. Spikes sprouted from his large arms, chest, and hips. He grew impossibly large. Transparent wings sprang from his back. He wielded a sword as long as his great body and ascended above Apollo's army.

Alexander grew to eight feet in height. His horned head came to a tall point that matched the sharp length of a spiked chin. His skin became exposed muscle. The heads of skeletons grew out of his back, and his large hands carried a scepter filled with the heads of skeletons that shot fire when he pointed it.

Kane's transformation trumped them all. He grew to more than ten feet tall. Hundreds of sharp horns grew out from his body. His head continued to transform from shark to something indistinguishable and terrifying. In-between the horns, hundreds of tentacles, more than eight feet long, reached out displaying the capability to choke the life from approaching soldiers.

At the command of each of their leaders, the combined covens, with the exception of my wolves, rose. One thousand vampire bats, filled the air. They descended upon the gold-armored, giant soldiers, ripping at their bared throats. Super-sized as they were, these soldiers appeared human in their ability to bleed. The soldiers fought back, slashing through the bats. The bats gnashed jugulars, feeding in a frenzy, taking many soldiers to their knees, as they too were torn apart. The enemy's super-human backup forces were more than a match for the bats. They ran forward, slashing through more than a hundred bats with their silver-lined swords and leaving them for dead.

Our vampire demon warriors moved forward, slashing, and mutilating their enemies. Alexander set an entire flank on fire with his scepter. Still, the enemy outnumbered us and continued to slaughter the bats with their deadly silver swords.

"RETREAT" filled the air, and the returning bats circled and screeched. I looked on in amazement as severed bat parts slowly reassembled — legs crawled back to bodies, wings flapped until they reached the proper socket, heads rolled back to find the right neck. Blood and spatter moved to re-enter its parent body. This reassembly was a sight to behold. The vampire bats transformed into giant demons, matching their coven leaders. "ATTACK!" was again shouted. Meanwhile, the unscathed bats morphed into giant winged dragons, breathing fire. They swirled over the marching soldiers and scorched more than a thousand of the enemy.

Apollo's backup archers carried silver bows. They were able to bring down several winged ones who burst into flames when hit by silver arrows.

The coven leaders morphed again into all manner of horrifying creatures. Were-jaguars. A giant T-Rex. Even a pterodactyl that spewed flaming blood over the majority of the enemy soldiers. The pterodactyl took a nose dive and floated no more than eight feet above hundreds of soldiers, instantly incinerating them. At this point, I could not tell one coven leader from the other apart. They continuously morphed each time they were wounded. Those that had morphed into were-jaguars took on enemy of like kind. Their giant bodies crashed against each other, and the earth shook with the shock of their clash. Some fell to the ground, pummeling each other. It reminded me of the time that Tommy, my little one from my human family, and I sat and watched *Godzilla vs. Rodan* on television. One gnashed a gaping hole in the shoulder of the other. Another ripped out the entrails of his opponent. I could only hope that our guys were winning.

Selene and I remained beside Brogio. My coven moved restlessly behind me. I could feel Scrawny's eyes trained on me still from afar. I wondered if he was planning to attack me, or to help with the escalating battle. I looked up at Brogio for some signal that my coven and I should enter the fray. Not taking his eyes from the battle, his words crept into my brain. "Not yet. You and I will wait for Apollo. If I fail to kill him, I need you to do so to protect Selene."

The giant T-Rex ran through the enemy with his mouth open, scooping up more than fifty armored soldiers, swords, bows, and arrows. Apollo stood on his chariot, surrounded by hundreds of his soldiers. He fired silver arrows into the T-Rex, but it was impervious to anything that Apollo could shoot at it. It bit down hard, then spit out heads, arms, legs, pieces of metal.

Apollo moved through the devastation of his army to within 50 yards of us. He emerged unscathed. He was magnificent in gold armor, blonde curls, and piercing sun-filled eyes, just as he had appeared in my dream. He reminded me of one of Tommy's comic book superheroes. He stood proudly in his horse-drawn, pure gold chariot. I had never seen anything as shining as this. It filled the night with its light, as if the sun fueled it. All the night creatures stepped away from it in fear of being scalded. The battle raged around him without touching him, or the soldiers near him. He appeared to be surrounded by an invisible barrier that he could activate or release at will. He marched forward, never taking his eyes from Brogio, who in almost invisible speed ripped out, with fangs and claws, the throats of every golden soldier between Apollo and himself. I stood in awe of both my Alpha and the god. The power of Apollo radiated from the human form he had taken. His beauty and confidence were blinding. His presence made everyone around him, except Brogio, look small and inadequate. And, with all his beauty, his presence was terrifying. His eyes, even filled with sunlight, projected evil intent. I could smell the evil, despite the spectacle.

In a gesture of supreme self-confidence, Apollo released his shield twenty yards in front of us. Two of our giant coven were-jaguars moved to attack him. With lighting speed, he cut them in half with his sun-filled silver sword.

In that moment, I knew that as powerful as my master was, he would never be able to defeat Apollo. I turned to my pack, *Follow me! Take him now!*

"No!" Brogio's scream ripped into my head.

YES! Was my reply as I willed myself forward. My paws moved as if I were swimming through waves of water. I pulled the power of my children into me, and together we broke Brogio's attempt to paralyze my body.

Instantly, Selene, who had been standing by me throughout the battle, called loudly to him. "Apollo, I am here! See me!" She threw off the heavy coat she had been wearing to reveal tight black pants and a silver sweater that clung to her every curve.

Apollo's concentration was momentarily broken. He stopped to look into her eyes and gaze upon her silvery beauty. That was the break that we needed. I forced my orders into the brains of my wolves, and my pack immediately morphed into black demons from hell. Their bodies grew to seven feet in length, with fangs of prehistoric length. Their hairless bodies sprouted horns from every pore. They spread out and ran around me, attacking the god from all sides. They were thrown from left to right, yelping and bounding back for more. The god tore off the front leg of one faithful child and tossed it aside, and still my pack refused to back down. My five converged on him, tearing at him with teeth, claws and horn, snarling, slashing, trying to bite, but unable to take him down.

However, they made a large enough distraction for me to strike.

I prepared to spring forward and fight Apollo to the death, when I felt a gentle hand on my head. It was Selene's. "Wait."

She passed me and walked forward, mesmerizing Apollo, who easily threw off my followers by tossing each one in the air. He stood in awe of her. She took several steps in his direction, nearing the confident warrior. He let down his guard and reached out to her. Not only his love of beauty, but his pride and arrogance gave us an opening. As she arrived at his feet, Brogio, who followed her, reached forward with his arms extended and pulled her behind him.

That was the cue I was waiting for. I sprung onto Apollo with all the power in my hind legs. I was instantly on his chest. In mortal form, he was vulnerable to me. My fangs sank deep into his throat. The sword he still carried in his right hand plunged and twisted into my stomach. I held fast, withstanding the searing pain. His twisting sword cut through me, ripping through my flesh. I saw my life flash before my eyes. It was Scrawny who rushed in to my defense as Brogio pulled Selene away from the fray. I felt Scrawny's thoughts as he circled around behind the god, surprising the soldiers at his back as he bolted through

197

them. He leaped on Apollo's back, sinking his fangs into the god's neck. A thunderous shriek echoed across the woods. The three of us fell to the ground. My venom, combined with Scrawny's, coursed through the god's human-like veins. Foaming and twisting, it raced through Apollo's beautiful human form until his body ceased to move.

I was lying face down in the grass with Apollo's sword piercing my belly. I could not crawl away to safety. I reached down inside for my last ounce of energy and lifted my head to watch as Apollo's human form began to dissolve like rapid rotting. My pack of demons reverted back to wolf form and began to snarl and bite at the air in frustration of my impending demise. Leander landed near my one legless progeny and offered him his blood to heal him. Scrawny, who lay next to Apollo's dissolving form, rolled over, stood, and tugged me away from the puddle of black, stinking oil that Apollo's body had left. A large, black stream of smoke emerged and lifted upward. The air filled with a wispy, raw voice. "Damn you! You will all die!"

EPISODE SIX
Kane

Scrawny pulled me by my collar from the oozing pile. I opened my eyes long enough to see into the depths of his.

If I cannot lead, then I will follow you. The one who has bested me is my master.

Selene's hands were soft on my head. "Stay still, Snow. Stay with us. Hang in there." She had a concerned tone to her voice.

I felt Brogio's strong hands on me as he silently pulled the sword from my side. The pain sliced through every nerve ending; blood spurted from my open wound. I could feel my body changing from demon to dog, making the pain even worse.

Scrawny moved closer and growled a warning.

I fought to stay conscious and reassure my fledgling child by invading his thoughts. *It is all right. They are my pack. He is my master. They are trying to heal me.*

199

I could see the battlefield from where I lay. Kane, who had continued to fight from the air above us, landed nearby and morphed back into human form. Realization spread across his face when he saw me on the ground. He dashed to me in a heartbeat. Examining me thoroughly, he bent and licked the inside and the outside of my gaping wound. The gush of blood ceased. The pain slowly calmed.

Brogio bit his wrist and force-fed me his blood. He lifted me from the ground, gently wrapped me in his arms, and carried me to the house, some one hundred yards away.

The screams from Apollo's dying army swirled around me. I felt myself fading into slumber. With my last thought before the darkness took me, I commanded Scrawny to obey Brogio until I returned. If I returned ...

*****

Selene's hand rested on my leg as she slept beside me. Light streamed through her bedroom window. I wondered how long I had gone into the darkness. Raising my head, I sniffed my shoulder and nibbled at my side where the wound had now disappeared. Not even a scar where Apollo's sword had pierced my flesh. Six pairs of golden eyes peered at me from the foot of the bed.

How long have I ...

Scrawny silently spoke to me. *Two days, my Alpha. We have been by your side, as has the silver woman.* His eyes shrewdly accessed Selene. *You healed. We all healed. Are we invincible?*

We can die, my children, but only by fire, or a wooden stake, or silver bullet through the heart. The stake must be made from a magical tree. I stood up on the bed and shook off sleep. Selene breathed softly and remained in slumber.

We are hungry. Their six voices sounded like petulant children cueing me to teach them what I knew. I tentatively climbed down from the bed. Cautious steps around the room assured me I was sound. My coven surrounded me, playfully nipping and wrestling with me on the floor. Then, I jumped up and ran out the door.

I'm feeling like myself again. Getting hungry too. Let's go hunting!

We hit the woods in our natural form and stalked our animal prey. I watched with pride as my young neophytes used the technique I had taught them to trap and take the blood from their prey. Scrawny, though not participating in my first lesson, appeared to have learned well from afar.

After gorging on wild boar, we sprawled under several large trees, and my mind turned to naming them.

I looked at Scrawny.

He snorted. *I already know. Scrawny. Not much of a name, but so it is.*

I barked my approval.

Next, my eyes fell on the large black wolf that I had thought would be their leader. His yellow eyes watched me expectantly. *I shall call you "Chase." You appear to always be after something!*

Chase sat up and barked. He fell over backwards and scratched his back on the acorns, leaves, and branches underneath him.

I moved on to my lanky, tall, dark brown child. One ear always seemed to flop over when he relaxed, giving him a playful appearance. Before I could give him a name, he dashed and scooted around the trees, in and out. Then, he turned and chased his tail. *Joker! I want to be Joker!*

I barked my approval. *So it shall be, Joker.*

My large light brown wolf lay at the perimeter of our resting place. He reminded me of a guardian. *You will be called Gaspar.*

He turned to me and bowed his head in acceptance. I sensed he would be a valuable part of our pack.

One gray wolf lay nonchalantly asleep on the forest floor in a blood coma. I willed him to look at me. *Shall I call you Sleeper?*

Sleeper? No! I am like thunder in battle! Do you not remember?

I thought for a moment. *Ah, yes. Then, you are Thor.*

Thor jumped to his feet and went crashing through the woods, making enough noise to scare off any prey that might have been available.

Enough, Thor! I get it!

That left the final wolf. His multi-colored coat had highlights of black, brown, gray, and even white fur. He was large and magnificent. The oldest of the pack, he was wise and had to have been a pack leader at one time. He sat back on his haunches and stared into my eyes. I answered him. *You are Fergus.*

Yes, you are wise.

So, Scrawny, Chase, Joker, Gaspar, Thor and Fergus – my progeny.

They all looked at me expectantly. *You are our pack master. We are yours to command.*

I thought it a heavy burden, indeed.

* * * * *

We returned to the front of the house as darkness fell, just in time to see the vampire covens preparing to leave. The coven leaders mulled around Brogio and Kane. Hundreds of remaining bats hovered in the surrounding trees. The air smelled of their sadness at the loss of hundreds of their brethren. I could only imagine how each coven master suffered during the days I lay unconscious and healing at the loss of their progeny who had suffered the true death. Young as my children were to me, I could not bear the thought of losing even one of them.

Leander stopped squarely in front of Brogio and searched his Alpha's eyes. "Are you sure, Master, that you do not want us to all stay a few days more?" A blonde lock of hair fell over one eye.

"No, Apollo is immortal, but he knows now that Selene stood by me in battle against him. I sense that it will be some time before he returns to torture us again."

Leslie, Ian, Joseph, and Alexander joined them. "We are hesitant to leave," Ian added. He threw a long slender arm around Leslie's waist and pulled her close to him.

Joseph stood back a bit, doing cartwheels around Alexander who laughed at the boy vampire's antics. Kane lingered around a tall redhead, one of Leslie's coven. He leered at her with obvious intentions to mate her at the next opportunity.

"Snow Blood and his coven will take up guard during the day. Nothing that you could do in the sunlight anyway. Go home and take my undying appreciation for all that each of you has given to me."

He motioned to the two men who had driven us here so many weeks ago. They stood aside holding a cart that contained numerous bottles of wine. They moved forward, and Brogio handed several bottles to each coven leader. "Take these. They are the most treasured of my vintage. Salute those we have lost as you drink it, and think of my undying love for each of you."

Leslie grinned and pointed at Brogio "I think he wants us gone so that he can bed the silver one without interruption." Her fingers tip-toed up Ian's broad chest.

"Be gone, all of you!" Brogio smiled and waved his hand in the air.

The bats that lined the trees rose in the air and flew away. Folding their wine bottles inside their long coats, each coven leader turned and left a blurred trail behind them as they moved at vampire speed away from us. Brogio and Kane stood looking after them for a moment.

I sat staring at my Alpha, my thoughts lingering on Leslie's words.

Brogio turned to me with a questioning stare. "Do you have something to say, Snow Blood?"

I sat back on my haunches. *I think it is time to make Selene your mate. Don't you?*

He scowled at me, frustration oozing from his every pore, like blood dripping deliciously from an open vein. "Mind your own business, vamp dog!"

I took up a momentary flea chase on my left paw, ignoring his withering stare.

Kane, surmising my taunt from Brogio's outburst, sputtered with laughter and wandered off into the house.

My coven will rest now during the dark hours. I led my pack into the house, and we all took up the beds that had been installed for us. Each of my coven selected one of the beds placed around the den near mine. I was at once asleep, but dreams filled with Artemis' oily voice plagued me. "Soon, Snow Blood. We have a deal. Soon you will be mine."

*****

I awoke abruptly. The hairs stood up on my neck. They were arguing. Their voices were distant, upstairs. I walked

205

to the window to find the night still upon us. My progeny slept the sleep of the undead. I followed my master's voice.

"Selene, stop torturing us. I need to possess you completely. I have waited ... forever." His voice revealed his pain.

"But the moment we are joined, will you turn me into ..." Her voice faltered.

"Into what? A monster like me?"

"Brogio, please, don't make this more difficult. I ... I'm not ready to be turned."

"But don't you see? It's the only way!"

"Why? Why is it?"

"You know why! She tricked us before and took you away from me!" I could hear him struggling with his words, his voice strident. "Apollo will never stop until he wins you for himself. If you are no longer ... virgin ..."

"No, I don't remember. That was your wife. I have no memory of it!"

"Why won't you believe me?"

I climbed the stairs in stealth mode and went to the slightly cracked door of Selene's room. My curiosity consumed me.

He stood next to her as she sat on the bed. Her shirt had been ripped, and the bed showed signs of a struggle. She stood abruptly, pulling her torn shirt over her heaving chest.

"I love you, but I will not be bullied into giving myself completely to you without proof that it is me you love. I won't be her substitute!"

He ran his hands through his silver hair and shook his fist at the ceiling. "You are not a substitute! You are my wife! Don't you think I would know that?"

"Then, why do I have no memory of us before I felt compelled to meet you? Why am I so drawn to you anyway?"

"Listen to yourself, Selene! Why do you think? Because you are MY ORIGINAL SELENE! Why do you not know it?" He took long strides to the door and yanked it open just as I bolted away.

"Snow Blood! What the hell?" His violet eyes turned red, and I froze in my tracks.

I heard arguing. Wanted to make sure you were all right.

"No, you were spying on us! Why?"

I just want to help you ... help you both.

"How will your eavesdropping help any of us?"

I couldn't tell him that Selene would be safe from Artemis if I kept my part of our bargain. *However I can.*

"Then stop snooping about and get some rest! I need you alert tomorrow." His footsteps appeared heavier than usual as he went down the stairs and out the front door.

Selene's sobs pulled at me. I wanted to retreat to my bed. Our friendship prevented it. I nosed her bedroom door open and trotted to her bedside.

Tears stained her pale cheeks with red blotches. I looked up. She sobbed harder at the sight of me. I gently leaped on the bed and curled up next to her. She immediately flung her arms around me and through ragged gulps questioned me. "Was it hard ... for you? What is it like ... to be a vampire?

Knowing she couldn't hear me, I put my chin on her hip and whined. I remained until she cried herself to sleep.

Fergus lifted his head as I crawled back into my plush bed. *This is something the humans must work out, my Alpha.*

Yes and no, Fergus. Yes and no.

*****

The air in the household reeked of tension at night. Brogio's pursuit to mate and turn his beloved into a vampire consumed us all. I took Scrawny, Chase, Joker, Gaspar, Thor and Fergus on nightly hunts to quench our thirst, and to get away from the toxic atmosphere. I forbade them to harm humans, so they had no comparison and seemed satisfied with the large game that we took down. Our days passed uneventfully, but we remained ever vigilant against the immortal Apollo, or other intruders who might try to take out Brogio and Kane while they slept.

My coven and I found rest in the wee hours of the morning before sunlight. After their nightly argument,

Brogio would slam through the front door in search of victims to satisfy his lust. One such night, I wrestled with sleeplessness. When Brogio slammed the front door, I got up and stared after him at the window until I watched him disappear into the woods.

I felt the discomfort before the voice came, slithering through my brain, calling me. It had been weeks since I had heard Artemis' whisper, and I felt a jolt at the sound of it.

"Snow, come to me. It's time."

The words pulled at my body. I looked back at my pack. They all were asleep.

"Come to me. To the field."

Before I realized it, my feet moved out the front door. I couldn't resist. Her pull on me was as strong as Brogio's. I walked as if in neck-high water and mud through the fresh snow that covered the ground, like a prisoner going to his execution. I found her in her field, an exact duplicate of the other two before it. Surrounded by snow-covered trees, she filled the clearing.

She created a circle of changing colors of light and shimmered just above the ground. Rabbits, deer, squirrels, and even a boar stood outside the light, frozen in awe of her. She beckoned to me, and I stepped inside her glowing circle.

"My Snow Blood. The time will be soon. You have done what you must for Brogio. Prepare to leave everything behind."

So soon? I have progeny that I must care for. I must protect my pack from Apollo.

"You need not fear Apollo as far as the others are concerned. His pride is wounded. He will leave your Alpha alone for now. He was humiliated in front of the one he prizes. It is you that worries me." She shimmered. Her light darkened.

I sat back on my haunches. *Why?*

"You are the cause of my brother's humiliation. You, not Brogio, you and your coven took him down." She reached out and touched my head. A shiver went up my spine.

Do you mean ... do you think he will come after me and my coven? I shifted my weight from one leg to the other in anticipation of her answer.

"Yes. And I must protect you. Say your goodbyes. Come back to me here in two days."

Two days! I need more time! I have children ... I can't protect them ...

"Enough! Two days at this time!" She faded and the light dimmed.

Wait! I need more time!

She shimmered and her light slowly faded and vanished. I stood surrounded by creatures that scattered without the protection of her light.

I pondered what I would do. I couldn't tell Brogio. He would try to fight for me. He would want to know why I had agreed to go. But, I had to protect my coven. Light footsteps alerted me, and I swirled to see Kane in human form glide out of the trees.

"So, my brother, she is calling in her chips?" The smirk on his face annoyed me. Ever since he had applied his healing licks to my back and wounds, we seemed to be able to communicate freely.

Why are you following me?

"Someone has to help keep you out of trouble." He wiped his long fingernails on what Brogio called his "foppish" jacket, and crossed his arms.

You can do nothing. She wants to take me in two days. I have to figure out how to protect my progeny!

"I heard. The sun will be rising soon. Let's go back to the house. Rest awaits me, but meet me here tomorrow night after sunset. I might just have a plan to help you."

He turned and walked into the trees until I could see him no longer. How did Kane think he could help me? I only felt more confused by his words.

*****

My appetite for blood and sleep left me while I waited restlessly for my meeting with Kane at sunset. I arrived early and sat sniffing the air, breathing in the essence of pine, juniper, and the last snow of winter. I would miss not being able to have the wind catch the hairs around my face. I sucked in the smell of the pine cones lying dormant under the surrounding trees. What kind of life would I have with a selfish, vain goddess who would most likely tire of me quickly?

I heard Kane's light footsteps and turned to meet the steady gaze of his dark eyes. His long, flowing black hair was pulled back in a knot. He had dressed in a silver grey jacket over black pants and a silver turtleneck. Brogio always said Kane dressed like a dandy.

Tell me of your ideas, Kane. I'm running out of time.

"Not ideas, my dog brother. A proposal." He swiftly removed his jacket, shirt, pants, and shoes and hung them on the branch of a nearby tree.

I don't get it. What are you doing?

"Wait. Hear me out. First, let me give you a demonstration."

Suddenly, Kane shrank before my eyes. His eyes met mine but changed from dark brown to steel blue. His face elongated, his nose became a snout. He sprouted hair all over his naked body. He had transformed into ... me! He had replicated me down to the hairs around my ears! He turned in a circle so that I could see all of him.

I don't understand. How did you do this? And why?

He morphed back to himself, held up a finger and smiled. "Wait." Next, he transformed into ... my Alpha. He was Brogio! He even smelled like Brogio!

What are you doing? And how is this possible?

Instead of offering an immediate answer, Kane morphed back into himself as a human. He redressed in his clothing and sat on a fallen tree trunk. He motioned for me to come near.

Kane, I don't understand. You are very talented, but why did you show me these powers?

"Ah, but my dear boy, let me clarify." He looked deeply into my eyes. "You don't want to go with Artemis and be her play thing. On the other hand, I am bored with this life."

I cocked my head at him and continued to watch him closely.

"Snow Blood, I have been in existence almost as long as Brogio. I bore easily. And, I have no Selene to burn over. Going with Artemis would be an adventure for me!"

I can't ask you to do that, my brother! And, why do you think she would accept you in my place? She's going to notice the difference.

"Look, she wants someone willing to play her little games. She said she could turn you into anything she wanted. You wouldn't be a willing partner, but I would be. I will show her how I can be you, or Brogio, who I know she secretly desires. I can be anyone, or anything else she wants. I could keep her entertained for centuries!" He jumped up, threw back his head, and roared. "It would keep me from being bored as well!"

But Brogio would never let you go. We all need you with us!

213

"No, that's where you are wrong. You see, when I get bored, I start to make mischief. I would screw with all of you – Brogio, Selene, you, your pack. You would come to hate me! Why do you think Brogio goes for a hundred years at a time without summoning me?" He sat back down and looked into my eyes. "Remember how we fought when I first arrived?"

But, I can't let you do this! Why would you do this for me?

"Don't you get it, dog? It's not for you. I want to do this." He stood again and walked in circles. "Well, maybe it's a little bit for you. You need to be here to help protect Brogio. I do care about him. But I can't keep watch for him during the day. None of his minions are as effective as you, and now your pack. And, you are more loyal to our master than everyone has ever been. Let me do this for you, and for him."

I sat in silence pondering his generous offer. I then stood and walked up to him, the top of my head almost touching his belt. I looked deeply into his eyes again and knew that what he said was the truth.

What will we tell Brogio?

"Nothing. Like I told you, he is used to me disappearing for long stretches of time. Besides, he is completely obsessed with Selene right now."

But what will happen when he summons you?

"At that point, there will be nothing he can do."

But I won't be able to hide the truth from him. I stood my ground.

"I repeat, at that point, there will be nothing he can do." He shrugged as if to say it was all settled.

And Artemis? How will we convince her?

"Leave it to me, Snow Blood. I will convince her that she is getting what she wants. I can be pretty persuasive when I want something."

＊＊＊＊＊

I wrestled with this course of action. It wasn't in my nature not to try and handle my own problems. But Kane was adamant. He appeared to look forward to it all.

I spent the rest of the night avoiding the house. I summoned my coven, and we hunted near the lake. We all slept in the woods, gorged on our blood feast, and then slunk home at sunrise. We took our positions outside the house. Scrawny took the back of the house near a large pine tree. I sat under a shade tree next to the front door that gave me good coverage of both the house and the wine cellar. The others positioned themselves under trees all around the house and winery.

When the sun was high in the sky, Selene joined me under the tree. In that moment, I wished I could communicate with her. I wanted to tell her that being a vampire hadn't been a bad thing for me. I wanted to share how I had resisted, but that I knew Brogio loved me, and that had made the difference.

215

She sat with her knees drawn up to her chest and one arm thrown over my neck, her fingers scratching at my right ear.

"I wish you could talk, Snow. I would want your counsel." She switched her fingers over to my left ear, and it felt so good that my left leg began to spasm.

A loud noise caused me to sweep the yard for intruders. It was probably just thunder, or a faraway car backfiring. I stood and turned to face Selene eye-to-eye. I concentrated as hard as I could to try and get through to her. My thoughts repeated a litany. *Yield to him. Yield to him. He loves you. This is the way he can protect you.*

I forced my thoughts into her mind, my stare mesmerizing her. The pupils of her eyes dilated, and I imagined she might have heard part of my message to her.

"You ... You want me to become one of you?" She scooted back away from me, her gaze never leaving mine. "Do you believe that I am his wife?"

I barked my response, and disbelief spread across her face. She stood abruptly, swaying as if she might fall. She steadied herself, raised her chin, and searched the landscape for some unknown point. "Very well, then. I will take your advice under consideration." She turned to go to the house, but I blocked her with my body.

I placed my head under her hand to show her my feelings, and her fingers buried into my fur and caressed my ears gently. Then, she took long strides up to the house.

When she reached it, she turned and smiled at me and slipped through the door.

I returned to my watchful post and spent the day in heavy thought.

*****

Night crept up the lawn and surrounded me. I ordered my pack to quench their hunger.

What about you? Scrawny turned with a question toward me.

Go on. I have things to tend to tonight. You can lead the coven in the hunt tonight. If I had to keep my promise to Artemis, I knew Scrawny would lead the coven.

He howled and ran, the coven all following right behind him.

I found Kane in the den with a glass of wine in his hands. Brogio was strangely absent.

"Snow, he's so frustrated. He took off and left the house as soon as we rose from our rest. He went out the backdoor to avoid Selene." He sighed. "I'm not sure why Selene has stayed. I guess it's all about love or lust. She wants to be with him. I feel sorry for her. Anyway, it's good that he's absent. We don't need to make excuses to meet with Artemis."

Kane, are you sure that you still want to go through with this?

217

"My boy, I've never been so serious. But, you know that if it doesn't work, you won't be able to say goodbye to Brogio. Being anywhere around him would give it away. If he wasn't so distracted right now, he'd be all over this in a heartbeat."

Yes. I know. I will meet you in the field at the required time. I turned to go, and then circled back. Walking up to Kane, I stretched my neck toward him and licked his hand, which rested on an arm chair. *Thank you, Kane. For being my brother.*

He lifted the same hand and placed it on my head. "It has been my honor, Snow Blood."

If this works, will I ever see you again?

"Who knows ... I hope someday, perhaps." He drained his glass and stood to refill it.

I crept out of the house quietly and wandered in the woods until it was time to meet Artemis.

*****

We stood together outside her circle of light. Kane had left his clothing in the woods and stood naked with me. I thought, if nothing else, this would pique her interest.

"Why have you appeared before me during this important moment, savage?"

Kane failed on an attempt to enter her light. "Let me enter your presence beautiful one, so that I might give you a gift."

The light swirled, expanded upward, and then changed to a pink hue. "A gift? Snow Blood, is this your attempt to go back on your word?"

"A gift, goddess. Not from Snow Blood, but from me. Snow Blood has come in good faith for the taking. But, before you take him, consider an exquisite alternative." Kane bowed with his words.

"Alternative? I want NO alternative. What tricks do you play, blood sucker!"

"Ah, but my lady, Snow Blood is a vampire too. Or have you forgotten that?"

"I have not forgotten, but I can make him into any image I want! We can be dogs together, lovers together, anything that I want!"

"Yes, but consider this. Do you want an unwilling mate whose heart will always be elsewhere, or do you want one who will be totally devoted to you?"

I squirmed on my haunches, waiting for the explosion I feared would come at Kane's words. Instead, the light darkened, then turned a brighter pink.

"I want what I want!" Artemis stomped her foot like a petulant child and swirled stirring the wind in the trees around us. Then she settled on me. "Snow Blood, what of our bargain?"

Kane interceded. "Please, Artemis, let me into your light so that I may show you what I can be for you."

"Very well. It won't hurt me to see what you propose." Her light shimmered silver, and Kane immediately stepped into it.

My heart skipped a beat. He's in! She's curious!

Kane stood before her, and the goddess commanded, "Show me."

Kane immediately transformed into the exact image of me.

Artemis instantly rose above him in her bubble of light, surprise written on her face.

Kane then jumped up and put his paw on her hand to pull her down. She followed. Then, he rubbed his (my?) body around her skirt, smothering her hands with licks and nibbles.

She chuckled with pleasure. Kneeling down, she inspected every inch of him as he eagerly licked her face every chance he got.

"It's amazing! You are exactly like Snow!"

Then Kane immediately stood on his hind legs, placing each of his paws on her shoulder as he morphed into Brogio. He took her in his arms and kissed her passionately. She responded, her light swirling and turning from silver to blue to pink and then a hot red.

Kane slowly released her. "I can be anything, or anyone you want me to be. Instead of forcing Snow Blood to become what you want, let me anticipate what you need and become it. Let Snow Blood go, and take me, for as long as you want. I am willingly yours."

"But why?" The goddess appeared confused and excited at once. "How can you do this?"

"In addition to the ability to heal others, it is my gift. Snow Blood can walk in daylight. Each of us has a gift, or two." He turned and became a gorgeous winged horse.

He was so beautiful that it took my breath away. Artemis giggled with delight. "I love Pegasus!"

Kane instantly transformed into his naked self and stood before her. "Don't you see? Because I am a creature of the night, as are you, we were meant for each other. You will take care of my needs, and I yours. In any way you want."

Her light expanded in shades of blues and pulled me inside. Yet, I had no fear. I felt somehow loved in an odd way.

She placed her hand on Kane's chest. "Become Snow Blood."

Kane instantly obeyed. Holding the exact replica of my red collar around his neck, she fixed her gaze on me. "I accept this proposal. Snow Blood, you are free of your obligation to me. Return to Brogio."

She knelt down to Kane the dog and wrapped her arms around him. He placed his neck over her shoulder and hugged her to him. Her circle of light glowed rosy pink and then red. Her eyes filled with delight. They began to swirl, the light turning into spectacular colors of pinks, reds, oranges. The brilliant colors made it difficult to see the outlines of their bodies. The circle rose and carried them into the sky. Then, they disappeared.

I stood in any empty field alone. It occurred to me that the goddess' concern for my safety had dissolved with her new fascination in the instant gratification that Kane could bring her. What shallow beings these gods were! At least I was free to return home.

Sadness permeated my bones. I had lost a good friend, but it was what he wanted. How could I ever repay him? I knew that somehow, some day I would find a way.

*****

"Kane! Kane?" Brogio walked through the den looking for his number one child. The sun was about to rise. "Where the hell has he gone?"

He told me to tell you he was bored. He's gone off to find adventure.

"Since when are you his messenger, Snow Blood? Why didn't he tell me himself?" Brogio glanced through the window as the sun began to streak orange across the sky.

An impulse. He said you'd understand.

He stared deeply at me, and I jumbled my thoughts, thinking of my pack, imagining Kane on a wild excursion with one of Leslie's progeny, the sexy one with the red hair.

"Why are you trying to block me, Snow Blood?" The sun slowly streaked through the windows. "Damn! We will discuss this later." He was out the door, smoke trailing behind him as he made his way to the cellar for the day. His speed prevented him from igniting before he hit the wine cellar door.

I sighed, then turned to find my coven staring at me with suspicion.

What? Get to your posts! I barked out mentally. *It's for the best. For all of us.*

As you wish, my Alpha. As you wish. Scrawny eyed me again as he led the others out into the rising day.

*****

As night fell, I took my pack into the forest to sate our thirst for blood. Two boars and a deer later, we all napped under our favorite trees not far from the house.

"Snow Blood!" My Alpha's voice seeped through every corner of my mind. "Snow Blood, I would speak with you now!" It would only be moments before he began to probe my mind and discover everything.

I was resigned to fess up to the truth about Kane. Standing and shaking thoroughly, I glanced at my progeny. *Stay here and relax. Enjoy your time in the woods. Brogio needs me. I will call if I need your help.*

I made it through the woods to the house. Grabbing the door handle with my paw, I pulled down, slid through, and then pushed the door shut with my body.

Selene was descending the stairs as I entered. She walked to the den and approached Brogio. He sat in his familiar arm chair, nursing a glass of blood.

I made myself small in a corner, where I could watch and listen but not be seen.

"May we talk?" She put a pale, beautiful hand on his shoulder.

Dressed in his usual black, he took her hand and stood to face her. "Always, my love."

"I ... I've been thinking about our ... discussions." She bit her lip and then lifted her chin defiantly.

"Yes, it is all I think about these days. It has clouded all my abilities." He sat and pulled her onto his lap.

She ran her fingers through his pale hair and stared deeply into his eyes. "I've made a decision."

I could see his shoulders tense up with her words. "And?"

"Your argument is convincing. I know that if I am to be with you that I need to be able to protect myself from harm." Her fingers walked up his chest. "If being what you are will cool Apollo's desire for me, then that is what I must do."

Brogio threw back his head and laughed heartily. Standing with her in his arms, he swirled her around with joy. He then stopped, lowered her feet to the floor, and look deeply into her eyes. "You will belong to me. In every way?"

"Yes, even Snow Blood believes in our history. After everything, *I believe in our past*." She smiled shyly.

His eyes pierced into hers, and pure joy spread across his handsome face. He smiled down at Selene. "Snow Blood? That devil. I owe him!" He picked her up again and began to run with her up the stairs, four steps at a time.

"Wait!"

Her voice halted him mid-step.

"Not here in the house. Our first time should be under the full moon."

My intensified hearing allowed me to hear her whispered words.

"If I am to be a creature of the night, let me be born there."

Brogio turned and carried her gently down the stairs and out the door.

I followed them. They went directly to Artemis' field! Could he have sub-consciously known this is where I had always met the goddess? Had I ever hid anything from Brogio? Did he know?

I slunk behind a stand of trees with a perfect view of them. Why I needed to witness their mating is unclear to me. Perhaps because I knew this would forever complete my Alpha. I felt joy for him.

"For centuries when Artemis kept you with her in the moonlight, I waited until the moon's rotation brought you to me. I knew you were there." He slowly removed the silver dress she had worn on their first date. "I waited for the three nights when your touch crested full in the night."

He removed his black clothing and dropped it on the ground. They both stood naked. They were beautiful – a pale, silvery glow surrounded them.

Brogio touched her long, silver hair gently. "I'd strip down in a spot such as this. It mattered not how cold or hot, I soaked in your embrace. Just as humans stand and bask in the sunlight, I stood and writhed with pleasure at your moonlight." Brogio spread her shimmering silver dress on the ground, then gently laid her down on it. "Sometimes your rotation was during the day, and I'd have to wait another cycle. Sometimes there would be a blue moon, and I'd have you twice in one month." He laid down next to her.

She put one arm around his neck and touched him gently with the other.

He gasped. "You who I called for. Still call for."

She slid her hand up and down the length of his body.

Brogio's words came in short gasps. "Over 200 moon cycles past since the last time I felt you with me. I'd thought your ardor waned. You'd tired of waiting and found another. Or that Apollo had finally won you back completely."

He rolled over on top of her, and she moaned.

"But now, to feel you. To have more than a phantom touch. Yet I know it's you. Holding you is a simplicity of my undoing. I want you Selene, I want you, and it scares me. I've never had you. What if all this time, what if those hands of yours bite through the layers of frost I've built? What happens when the heat of your love touches my heart? Do

I incinerate to dust? Take me, Selene. I am paralyzed with duty and repetition of endless nights."

The scene was too intimate, too personal, but I couldn't leave.

"I am here, which means it's a full moon." Selene raised her chin. "You have wanted me for a thousand years. So take what is yours to keep."

Their love making was slow and beautiful. They kissed every part of each other. Before they consummated their love, he raised himself above her and stared into her eyes. "Tell me that you remember. Search some deep part of your mind to remember when we first met."

His will and his love for her seemed to compel her. A glimmer of realization spread across her face. She cried out, "I remember! I remember. Oh, my poor love, what you have suffered for me!" When he could hold back no longer, he plunged himself into her. His words came out in forced breaths. "My gods, I love you!"

Her cries of pleasure joined his and mingled with her words of love for him.

I wish I could have known such joy from mating.

My Alpha surprised me in their moment of joy. Brogio's face contorted, his fangs descended, and with one quick movement, he bit into her neck. Selene fought against him with her fists, crying out, shocked by the surge of pain that invaded the ecstasy of their love-making. Brogio held fast and sucked until she stopped fighting him. Then, she stopped moving.

The sky suddenly filled with lighting and thunder! The wind stirred the trees almost lifting the mated couple from the spot with its strength. The gods knew what was happening and rang their displeasure!

My Alpha quickly bit into his wrist and drizzled his blood into her mouth. The wind blew harder, and the trees began to bend even more. Minutes ticked by as Brogio held onto her and watched her intently, keeping his wrist placed over her mouth. Selene's limp form slowly stirred. She tentatively took hold of his arm and began to suck. Moments later, she arched her back as Brogio's blood infiltrated her body. The intensity of her feeding escalated. Brogio appeared in ecstasy again as she drank hungrily from his wrist. He instantly pulled her to her feet and kissed her passionately, blood running down both their faces. He picked his bride up, his wife at last, and twirled her around. Raising her to the heavens, he screamed, "Mine! She is mine forever!"

Lighting struck the trees, splitting many in half. Rain began to pelt them, and the wind moved it sideways, smacking them with the force of a hurricane. Unmovable, Brogio held onto his beloved, defying the gods. He lowered her and encircling her in his arms, threw back his head, his laughter ringing upward into the sky.

Selene's body shook in spasms as she began to transform. Brogio held her close, shielding her from the pelting wind and rain. But, even in her struggle with the transformation, Selene's voice joined his. "We are free!"

I threw back my head and howled at the moon. My coven slowly crept out from the trees behind me and joined me in celebration of my master's triumph.

THE END

Next in this series:

Snow Blood: Season 2 (A Vampire Mystery Thriller)

As dark forces close in on Brogio and his beloved children, the end of all vampires could come from a single blow at any moment.

When Kane sacrifices himself to save Snow Blood, the pack believes he is truly lost forever. After the devastating loss, a new ever-present threat of destruction surrounding Brogio, the original vampire, threatens his kindred.

While the pack stands guard watching for predators on the outskirts of Brogio's winery estate, Snow Blood discovers Selene is keeping secrets from Brogio. This deception and Selene's rapidly growing strength and independence could create a rift between the father of all vampires and his mate.

Snow Blood again helps hold their love together as he tries to protect them from the approaching evil. At the same time, Snow Blood suspects that Nova, the beautiful female wolf that attracts him in the forest, is part of a sinister plot to destroy his master … but he can't resist her power over him.

>>> Continue the Adventurous Paranormal Series

Universal Amazon link: http://mybook.to/SB2

Other Titles by Carol McKibben

If you liked reading from the perspective of a dog, you might like *Luke's Tale: A Story of Unconditional Love* by Carol McKibben...or Carol's inspirational drama, *Riding Through It.*

About Carol McKibben

Carol's love of animals, especially dogs and horses, is obvious in everything she writes. When Carol isn't feeding her horde of canine rescues, she's out riding her beloved Friesian on the plains of Texas. Her love of animals leads her to write through a dog's eyes. Carol's message is clear. "If a dog can love us unconditionally, why can't we do the same with each other?" And, her paranormal stories are often filled with characters that might be the most difficult to love.

Carol's writing career began at 14 years of age when she started telling her stories to Labrador Retrievers, Basset Hounds, and any stray that happened by. It wasn't long before people stopped to have a listen as well. Now, Carol writes for people and speaks to large audiences, dogs included.

Contact Carol at http://www.carolmckibben.com or join her at https://www.facebook.com/CarolMckibbenAuthor

www.ingramcontent.com/pod-product-compliance
Lightning Source LLC
Chambersburg PA
CBHW051457170626
46811CB00002B/517